GLOAMING

PROLOGUE

The great, rambling mansion-house of Landricourt stood quiet and empty, for the winemakers had finished their labour and gone home. All save one, who lingered in the cooling halls, her footsteps echoing in the hushed silence of the twilight hours. She loved the crumbling stone walls and the great windows, bare now of glass, through which the warm summer breezes drifted softly through the corridors. At this time of the year, the scent of rose hung heavy upon the air, so thickly floral that it grew almost cloying. The winemaker lingered near the long, empty windows of the long gallery, grateful for the cool, evening wind that brought respite from the clinging heat of the day.

It pleased her, when she walked there alone, to cast her mind back and back, through years of lost time, to the days when Landricourt was new. She imagined, as best she could, the elegance of the wood-panelled walls, when they had been whole and

1

intact; the grandeur of the house's winding stone staircases, sound and adorned with statuary; its great, imposing windows, glittering with panes of glass. A tapestry remained, here and there, though they hung in ragged shreds, naught left of them but a glimpse of the vivid colour that must once have flooded these abandoned halls. Some furniture lingered, a mismatched array evocative of Landricourt's long history: the great, heavy oak table that stood in the hall was largely untouched by time, while the chaise longue that lingered in the drawing-room had lost most of its exquisite amber silk upholstery, and none now dared to recline upon its fragile mahogany frame.

She had been gathering rose petals all afternoon, and when she had gazed her fill at the long gallery, and wandered through the decayed beauty of the drawing-room, she bore her two wide trugs down to the cellar, and emptied their contents into the vat that stood waiting. Others had already filled it half full, and on the morrow, the process of preserving the pale, delicate petals as rosewater would begin. She would have lingered longer in the cellar, for it was cool and dark where the day had been too bright and too hot. But the aroma of rose filled the confined space, too pungent, and she made her escape. At least twilight had carried away the glare of the sun, giving her tired eyes some respite.

She turned from the vat full of petals, and from the stone jars filled with the produce of weeks prior, and set out to return to the narrow stone staircase that had brought her into the depths of the house. Her work done, she had little excuse to linger any longer, and duties awaited her at home.

But as she set her foot upon the first of those

steps, wincing at the ache in her calves that protested against the forthcoming climb, a glimmer of light caught her eye. Prominent in the twilight-darkened cellar, the light was silvery and strange, and instinctively she turned towards it. It glimmered again, beckoning her some way down a shadowy passageway she had seldom had cause to explore before, and at last through an arched doorway whose door was long since lost.

The light glittered, turning from silver-pale to faintly blue, and — somehow — it came from the far wall, a wall that was naught but bare, unadorned stone. No lantern hung there, no torch, no window.

She approached, curious and puzzled. It would not be the first time that strange things had happened at Landricourt; the winemakers sometimes shared tales amongst themselves, little anecdotes of strange happenings and peculiarities. But she did not recall that anyone had yet mentioned a light like this, as pale and tantalising as the stars, its presence here incomprehensible.

Upon the wall hung a mirror without a frame. It hung by no visible means, the glass flat against the stone, and dark; so much so that she had not seen it from the other side of the room. It could scarcely be distinguished from the wall at all, save only when that glimmer came.

And there it came again, and winked out.

Like a pale torch flaring in the distance, its intermittent comings and goings resembled that of a lantern held by someone who passed, periodically, behind a tree or perhaps a pillar. Her hand stretched forth, only half voluntary, and when her fingers met the glass it gave beneath her touch in a way that cold, hard glass should *not*.

She thought she heard the distant sound of bells upon the air, and a note or two of a melody sung in high, strange voices.

And then she was no longer in the twilit cellar, and her half-formed wishes of a quarter of an hour before were abruptly given her. For she stood somewhere else — somewhere new, but familiar. She would have said she had not moved at all; that the sensation of falling, the momentary disorientation she had experienced, had all occurred inside her own mind, and signified nothing. The cellar-room in which she now stood was identical, in all its particulars, to the one that she had left.

Except that the light was wrong. A moment ago, she had stood shrouded in the deepening shadows of twilight, the cellar almost full dark around her. *This* cellar-chamber was bright with the soft daylight that streamed through its single, high-positioned window, so golden a glow that she would have placed the time at high noon.

The mirror was gone.

A few brisk steps carrying her to the door, she saw that the passageway was the same one down which she had walked only a few minutes before, or it *looked* the same. Only now it was neat and clean and well-swept, and flooded with light.

Quickly, she half-ran along that passage and up the stairs, and thence through a maze of passages and halls and chambers which she knew as well as she knew her own home; only *this* Landricourt was not ruined at all. Tapestries hung against pristine walls; carved wooden panels were well-kept and polished; everywhere there were drapes and rugs and furniture, and though it struck her, on the very edge of her flustered awareness, that they were of a style she had never before seen, and could never have dreamed, they were distinctly whole. The only mark of familiarity about the place was the occasional gap in the ceiling, through which an array of invasive rose-vines had determinedly crept. But these blooms were not silver or even white; they were pink and crimson and violet, a range of hues not seen at Landricourt in living memory.

She was not alone, either, for she passed men and women clad in raiment equally outlandish. They moved as quickly as she herself, only with purpose rather than fear, and paid scant attention to her hurried flight through the halls. Their garb was simple, their movements brisk, efficient; were these guests, residents or servants? She could not tell, and none paused to address her, nor gave her opportunity to ask. They did not seem even to see her.

When she arrived at last at the long gallery, she found it filled with people full strange to look upon, their garb the finest she had ever seen. Though it was broad daylight, somehow, in this place that was *other,* they were drinking a rich wine, and there was much laughter and merriment among them. These were the voices she had heard singing, perhaps.

For some time they did not notice her, and she began to wonder whether, in addition to her involuntary translocation, she was also turned invisible. But when at last one of them glanced her way — a gentleman of some age, she judged from his silvery-white hair, his coat the colour of plums in red wine — she found herself fixed with a stare neither welcoming nor otherwise.

'Ah,' he said at last, and she could discern nothing from his colourless tone.

Where was she? This was not *her* Landricourt. She was come, somehow, to a vision of the past — the past it *must* be, by some means beyond her comprehension. But who were the folk who dwelled here, and who gazed upon her with at least as much curiosity as she beheld them? For the faces of all in the gallery were turned towards her now, and she felt obliged to make a trembling curtsey, mindful, among such magnificence, of the stained and much-mended state of her cotton petticoats.

She wished in her secret heart that she had never wished at all, for she was alone in this Landricourt of strangers, and how was she ever to return home?

'Your name,' said the gentleman in the plum coat. He was not peremptory, but nor was he kind, and to her regret her discomfort caused her to stammer as she answered: 'I am c-called Oriane, Seigneur. Oriane Travere.'

His pale eyes narrowed as she spoke, his gaze sharpened upon her. Did she imagine an increase in alertness, an air of suppressed excitement about him? He looked at her closely; her face, her hair, her clothes, all came under his scrutiny. At last he said: 'And where have you come from, Oriane Travere?'

'Landricourt,' she whispered. She did not know how to explain, did not expect to be believed; how could she tell these strange, grand folk that she had come from some other Landricourt, a ruined one, which even now was sunk in the twilight of the Gloaming?

But she did not need to, for at her words his face cleared, and again he said: 'Ahh.'

PART ONE

MARGOT

CHAPTER ONE

The day was warm for hard work, and Margot De Courcey hitched her green cotton skirts a little higher, tucking folds of the fabric into the waistband until the hems rose above her knees. She spared a blush for propriety's sake, but only a fleeting one, for who was to see her, save those employed in a similar labour? And every one of the winemakers of Landricourt wore their skirts the same way, today.

The summer was well on its way towards the fall of the leaves, and the air was thick and close. Margot had made her way as far as the dining-room, where the empty windows allowed only occasional wisps of a sluggish breeze to touch her damp skin. The roses had come in through the ceiling in this part of the rambling old house, and by now the thicket of thorns and bright, burnished leaves had claimed two of the walls and half of a third. All summer long they had been abundant with fat, heavy blossoms, their translucent petals hovering somewhere between silver and white; pale like the moon, folded around a clear glimmering heart like the wrappings of some promised gift. Such roses only grew at Landricourt. Some of them flourished still, but many had bowed their majestic heads and spilled their petals all across the dining-room floor. Only the hearts remained, and these plumped and fattened as the days passed, forming round, polished hips fragrant with a tantalising scent all their own.

These Margot was engaged in gathering, her hands clad in thick leather gloves against the prickling thorns. It was a shame to wrest them from their stems, she always thought; they glittered faintly, as though a mote of starlight slumbered somewhere within, and she felt like a thief stealing nature's finest jewels. But they were succulent and fragrant, and the wine made from these fruits of autumn was beyond compare.

'They are a gift,' Maewen Brionnet had once said, and she had been a winemaker at Landricourt for years beyond counting. 'Shall we leave them to rot, ungathered? Tsh! Such would be a crime.'

It sometimes fell to Margot to cut the roses from their stems before they had chance to wither, for it was also tradition that the petals should be pressed and distilled into rosewater, and this added to the brew. Where these traditions had come from, no one knew; nor who had been the first to harvest the strange, moon-pale roses of Landricourt and craft them into wine. It was only known that this was done, year upon year, and under Maewen's direction the process had continued uninterrupted since before Margot's birth.

It must be growing late, Margot felt, and even as she formed the thought the song began: a low, wordless humming, Adelaide's rich voice leading the others. The Quincy family had always led the song, and Adelaide was a true daughter of theirs. For a few moments Margot merely listened, for Adelaide's voice was like warm, rich chocolate mixed with honey — if her glorious notes could be likened to anything earthly at all. When Margot's ears had drunk their fill of the melody, she lifted her own, less spectacular voice in her accustomed harmony. There were never words to the eventide song, but all knew the melody — even if its source was as lost to time as the tradition of wine-making at Landricourt.

The chimes came, melding with the music so perfectly that Margot struggled to make them out at all. One chime, two, three — grand, ringing sounds which echoed across the whole of Vale Argantel, emanating from the very skies.

A fourth resonant chime announced the arrival of four o' clock, and, as was the way of things, the Gloaming swept across the valley. The sun dimmed and faded, lingering only as a faint, muted presence upon the far horizon. Shadows crept out of the corners and danced across the dining-room, and what light remained turned as silvery as the stars.

The sun took most of the day's fierce heat away with it, and Margot wilted with relief. She clambered down from her perch atop an aged wooden step-ladder near the grand double-doors, holding her skirts carefully to keep her harvest of rosehips from spilling to the floor. Maewen had given her a basket the week before, a lovely woven thing more than capacious enough to hold many a rosehip. But Margot found it cumbersome, and preferred to continue using a fold of her skirt, turned up at the hem to form a cloth bag.

She regretted this a moment later, when a sudden hollering at the door caused her to start so severely that she dropped her skirt altogether. Her rosehips bounced and rolled away all over the floor, and Margot was left to curse both her own clumsiness and that of the visitor as she chased after them. She loved the evensong; it soothed and transported her, perhaps rather too much.

'I suppose you have brought something, Master Talleyrand?' she said tartly, for the noisy young man who had upset her harvest was Florian from the emporium in town. In the doorway he stood with his hands in his pockets, a flush staining his brown cheeks. He had got flour onto the tan cotton of his waistcoat somehow, and wisps of grass stuck out of the sage-green thicket of his hair.

Raucous he might sometimes be, but he was not boorish, for he flushed with dismay at the results of his too-eager greeting and hastened to help Margot collect them all up. 'Sorry,' he mumbled, and by the time all the pale rosehips were gathered and placed in Maewen's wicker basket, he was as red and perspiring as she.

Margot straightened her aching back with a wince, feeling far older than she ought at her relatively youthful age. Working all day in the heat had its deleterious effects; that must be her excuse. 'Well, what is it?' she prompted, when Florian seemed disposed only to stand there and observe her discomfort in silence.

'Actually, Seigneur Chanteraine requests your presence.' Recovering his composure, Florian said this with a bow, as though he were inviting her to attend a dance rather than to attend upon his employer at a moment's notice.

'I shall come at once,' she replied with a small sigh, for she had hoped to go directly to one of the streams behind Landricourt and wash away the day's aches and grime. But a leisurely walk home through the cool of the Gloaming would be pleasant enough. 'Why is it that I am wanted there?' she enquired. The request had perhaps come from Sylvaine, Seigneur Chanteraine's daughter and her occasional friend.

'He asks that you bring a bottle of the new season's rosewater.'

'I?' This was curious. 'Why does he not direct such a request to Oriane? She is his usual aide at Landricourt, is she not?'

'He did in fact ask for her at *first*, but I am told there is no sign of her today. I could only find Madame Brionnet, who sent me in search of you instead.' He added, with his swift grin, 'I found her at the top of the south-west turret, all used up for the day. I didn't know that snoring was a component in the evensong.'

Margot felt a moment's chagrin, for while she had been breaking her back in the dining-room, Maewen had been resting at her ease in a breezy tower-top! But the feeling melted away soon enough, for Madame Brionnet rarely allowed her age to slow her down. Instead, she laughed. 'Only if it is suitably melodic snoring, in keeping with the harmony.'

'It was, of course,' said Florian, undoubtedly with more gallantry than truth.

'Help me carry this basket,' she pleaded, for though she was strong she was weary, and Florian made a fine picture of boundless energy. He fell to the task willingly enough, and accompanied her through the rambling old mansion as she went in search of the rosewater. They left the basket in the main hall, with the rest of the day's harvest; a fine medley of containers was already deposited there, all brimming with rosehips.

Madame Brionnet stood over them as superintendent, and fixed Florian with a gimlet eye as he passed.

'I have said nothing, ma'am,' he assured her, mendaciously and in a loud whisper.

'I am sure there is nothing of which to speak,' said she stiffly. To Margot she added: 'Take two bottles of the water, my dear, and quickly. Seigneur Chanteraine may be pleased to have a little to spare.'

Maewen's eagerness to oblige the Chanteraines did not surprise Margot, for it was an attitude shared by many in Argantel. She hastened to obey the directive, glad to have Florian to assist her, for the great clay bottles were large and bulky and she did not feel equal to carting more than one of them across the valley.

As they left Landricourt in the deep twilight, the roses woke up around them, stretching their sparse petals under the soft, blue light. Their hearts swelled and shone, drinking up the effulgence, and Margot knew that when she returned in the morning there would be many more to collect. It was raining a little, though the sky was clear, and the distant strains of long-lost melodies drifted upon the wind.

Vale Argantel was not large. Landricourt was built against the downward slope of the hillside to the far west of the valley. The town of Argantel nestled in the centre, at the valley's lowest point. It was a safe spot, protected from high winds by the steep-sloping hills that rose all around it. Mist gathered in the early mornings and was slow to lift, clinging to the stone cottages and grey brick townhouses in a soft, white shroud.

Several small shops clustered around the central square. Arnaud Morel's bakery was famed for the excellence of its bread, freshly baked every morning; Heloise Guillory made gowns and coats all day long in the establishment beside; Osmont Charron and his wife Nolwenn sold the fresh produce grown in the fields that covered half of Vale Argantel. But chief among them all was Chanteraine & Daughter, a shop central to the needs of all Argantellians. No one could say where old Pharamond Chanteraine and his daughter Sylvaine procured their dazzling array of wares, the likes of which were seen nowhere else. Nor could the emporium's proprietors be drawn upon the subject. When asked, Pharamond merely shook his head in his mild way, and smiled a small smile, while Sylvaine could be relied upon to raise a single brow, and stare down the asker in formidable silence.

Margot had long since stopped asking, for though Sylvaine and she were approximately of an age with one another and had long been friends, on this topic the younger Chanteraine steadfastly refused to be drawn.

As Margot and Florian trudged through the rear door of Chanteraine & Daughter, out of breath and more than ready to set down their burdens, Margot was disappointed to find no Sylvaine there. Seigneur Chanteraine presided over the shop's counter; he could be heard selling a peach and clover cordial to Madame Courtney, his deep, mild voice instantly recognisable. Once madam was satisfied — and this took a few moments more, for she was unable to resist the additional purchase of a bar of wild thyme soap on her way out — Chanteraine came into the back room, and greeted Margot and his assistant with his customary courtesy. If he felt surprised at finding Margot there instead of Oriane, he concealed it with admirable aplomb, though he did direct one swift, keen look at Margot which she did not know how to interpret.

For all Pharamond's exquisite manners, he could sometimes make an imposing figure. He was unusually tall, even for a man, and but little diminished by advancing age. His hair might be grey through-and-through, but it was still thick and shining, framing a grave face lit by bright blue eyes. He was never given to chatter, but the quality of this particular silence did not reassure Margot, and she found herself blurting out: 'Oriane would have come, Seigneur, I am sure of it, were she not... indisposed.'

'Indisposed?' he repeated, one white brow lifting in enquiry.

'She has not been seen at Landricourt today. I believe she must be ill, and—'

'Has anybody gone to enquire after her?'

'—and I am on my way to call on her this moment,' finished Margot.

'If she should be in need of anything,' he answered, 'you will send word?'

Margot understood what he had not said: that he would be pleased if she would find Oriane in want of something — anything, no matter how trifling — so that he may receive news of her condition, but without any trace of impropriety attaching to the exchange. Seigneur prescribed to the old ways, and could never be persuaded that he might express a gentlemanly interest in Oriane Travere without incurring the opprobrium of the townspeople.

'You may expect it, Seigneur.'

Chanteraine made her a slight bow, his bright blue eyes flicking to Florian. 'Attend Demoiselle De Courcey, Florian. And you will carry with you a little gift for her, if you please. A...' He paused, perhaps undecided as to the nature of the gift he felt he might reasonably offer. He excused himself, and disappeared back into the shop for a few moments. When he returned, he bore two items in his large hands: a tiny, delicate glass bottle filled to the brim with a pale gold liquid, and a tiny book bound in peacock-blue silk, a length of violet ribbon fluttering from between its pages. 'With our compliments,' he said, handing both to Florian. 'The elixir will prove restorative, I hope.'

He did not explain the book, and the brief glimpse Margot received of its cover revealed only that it had no words of any kind printed upon its spine.

'Make haste, Florian,' said Chanteraine, and Florian made a hasty bow.

'We go with all possible speed, Seigneur.'

CHAPTER TWO

'You had better give me one or other of those,' said Margot, having watched Florian trudge the length of the Waldewiese with the book clutched in one hand and the fragile glass bottle swinging jauntily from the other.

He shot her an amused look. 'I will not drop them, Margot.'

She eyed the bottle with misgivings she did not attempt to hide. He had hold of it by its slender neck, and she did not like the way the bottle swayed back and forth with the rhythm of his long steps.

'Very well,' he said. 'If it will make you feel better.' He gave the bottle into her care, and she immediately took hold of it with both hands, cradling it gently. She was fascinated to find that the glass was warm to the touch.

'You are not curious as to the nature of the book?' she asked later, when silence had reigned between them for a few minutes.

'Excessively.'

Which was to say that he had no intention of satisfying his curiosity, or hers. She sighed inwardly, for the contents of the Chanteraine Emporium were known for their tendency towards rarity, peculiarity and a strangeness which sometimes seemed almost magical.

Oriane's little house was on the very edge of the town of Argantel, nothing standing between her cottage and Landricourt save the gentle upward slope of the valley, thick with grass and clover. A mere ten minutes brought Florian and Margot to Oriane's blue-painted front door, which stood closed tight against the balmy eventide breeze. No lights shone within.

'Perhaps she is asleep,' said Florian, and rapped gently upon the nearest window. When nothing came of this tentative advance, he rapped more loudly upon the door.

Margot did not answer, for her attention had been drawn elsewhere. Nothing ought to be visible of Landricourt at this distance, and at this hour of the day; the Gloaming clad the great old house in deep, impenetrable shadow. But there *was* something there: a faint, white light, glittering like a star. It could not be a star in truth; it hung far too low, and besides, it was yet too early in the day for the stars to emerge. What, then, could it be?

'Florian—' she began, but stopped, for as she spoke the light winked out and left the horizon in darkness.

'What is it?' said he.

She shook her head. 'I thought I saw…nothing. If Oriane is asleep, perhaps we ought not to disturb her?'

'Seigneur will want his report. And the door rattles.

I think it is not locked.'

'Seigneur Chanteraine cares for Oriane. If she is ill, he will not wish for her repose to be disturbed merely to allay his own concern.'

Florian glanced uncertainly at the book he held. It was small enough to fit into the palm of his hand, and looked dwarfed there.

'If the door is unlocked, perhaps we might leave these in her kitchen?' Margot suggested. 'She will find them when she wakes, and I am sure she will know who to thank for them.'

Florian remained uncertain, but he agreed to Margot's proposal. The front door of Oriane's cottage opened directly onto the kitchen, and thither they crept, careful to place down Pharamond's offerings without making such noise as might wake her. The house was fully dark.

They turned immediately to leave, but Margot hesitated upon the threshold. She did not like to leave without seeing Oriane, any more than Florian did. And the unlocked door disturbed her.

'Perhaps I will just look in on her,' she proposed. 'A mere moment, no more. I need not wake her.'

'If she is very ill, she may need Doctor Davinier,' Florian agreed.

This decided, Margot turned back from the door. She suffered a moment's confusion in the tiny hall, or she could not remember which of the three other doors there led into Oriane's bedchamber; she had visited the cottage only once or twice before, and not for some time.

But by luck or good fortune, her hand alighted upon the correct one, for upon opening the door, she discovered the curtains to be undrawn; the low, silvery-blue light of the Gloaming illuminated a small bed neatly tucked up with rose-coloured blankets.

It was empty.

'She is not here,' said Margot in confusion.

Florian busied himself with searching the other chambers, tapping politely upon each door before entering. There came no reply, and he returned swiftly from each new exploration, shaking his head.

'She is nowhere in the house? Where, then, can she be?'

'Perhaps she has already seen the doctor,' suggested Florian, 'and been taken somewhere.'

Taken somewhere? 'If so, then she is gravely ill indeed.' Margot felt a flutter of alarm. 'We had better see Madame Davinier at once.'

'I will return to the Emporium,' Florian said. 'Seigneur Chanteraine will wish to be told.'

'Not yet. We have nothing to tell, save that she is not at home. Let us receive the doctor's report, first.'

Florian made no objection to this, and the two quickly left the silent and dark cottage. Though not without a small delay, for on the way back through Oriane's tiny, neatly-kept kitchen, Margot observed something she had not noticed before.

There stood a sturdy rocking-chair in one corner of the kitchen, directly by the hearth. What Margot had taken for a blanket thrown over the back was no such thing, for it gave a strange glimmer in the half-light — a glister not unlike the misplaced star that had shone, briefly, over Landricourt.

'Hold a moment,' she told Florian. Quickly, she lit the modest candle that stood waiting upon the oaken table and held it nearer the bundle of fabric. This would not do; all she saw was a blossoming of colour

— mauve — and an intensifying of the silvery glimmer. She gave the candle into Florian's hands and, carefully, picked up the gossamer folds.

She held a gauzy coat, of such lightness it barely weighed anything, though she lifted it high. It was a strange thing, for the sweep of gossamer resembled a pair of folded moth's wings, with flimsy sleeves attached to the rest only by a set of fluttering ribbons. Never had she seen its like; it could not be further removed from the simpler garb of cotton and linen and wool that the folk of Argantel customarily wore, sometimes enlivened by a rustle of silk.

'How curious a thing,' she murmured.

'One of my master's oddities, perhaps,' suggested Florian.

'Oh? Have you seen such a garment at the emporium?'

'No,' he admitted. 'Never quite like that.'

Where had Oriane come by such a thing? For its delicacy alone proclaimed it a costly garment, and the wages of a winemaker were far from princely. And there was that glister besides, which came from intricate embroidery tracing the shapes and markings of the moth wings. It drank in the light of Florian's candle and threw it out again, twice as intense and eerily moon-pale.

Margot laid the pretty coat down again, feeling oddly troubled by its presence. What harm could come of a mere coat? It was only Oriane's absence that unsettled her, she told herself. Were it not for that, she would have admired the coat exceedingly, and felt no flicker of unease.

A visit to Madame Davinier, who lived quite on

the other side of Argantel, established not only that she had issued no orders for Oriane to be cared for outside of her home; the doctor also denied having seen or heard from Oriane at all.

They found her at home in her study, shown there by a servant only slightly more elderly than she. The doctor sat hunched over her modest desk, the meagre glow from a single lamp casting back the evening gloom. 'Travere?' said Madame Davinier, looking up from her book in mild confusion. 'No, no. I have not been called to attend upon her since the winter.' She blinked brown eyes in blank incomprehension. 'Is she unwell? I will come this moment.'

In so saying, she was already jumping out of her oak-carved chair and reaching past the shelves of leather-bound books for the capacious black bag that held all the tools of her trade.

'No, no!' cried Margot. 'She is not unwell. That is, we are not sure.'

'You are not sure?' Madame Davinier slowly set down her bag again, her gaze darting from Margot to Florian and back in puzzlement.

'She is not at home,' Florian supplied. 'And she has not been seen at Landricourt all day.'

'Strange,' said the doctor. 'But she is caring for another who is sick, perhaps, or engaged upon some other urgent task.'

This was quite the possibility. 'Depend upon it,' said Margot as they left the doctor's house, 'Oriane is with her mother, or a neighbour who is sick. You know how kind a heart she has.'

'With Seigneur's help, she will be the more quickly found,' suggested Florian.

'I would not wish to worry him unduly.'

'Why do you suppose he would be unduly worried?'

Margot could not explain, for her concern was based on nothing more distinct than the alert, intense look about Pharamond Chanteraine as he had spoken to her of Oriane. 'As you wish,' she said instead, for Florian must know his employer better than she.

Her misgivings were soon proved well-founded, for the moment Seigneur Chanteraine heard their news, he lost all his customary air of quiet serenity. The hour was growing late and he had closed the emporium for the night, but he lingered still in the stores at the back, checking the stock for the morrow. He set down his pen, looked long at Margot — who spared a thought to wish that he would not, for her long labours followed by her search for Oriane had left her in a state of some disorder — and demanded, 'Tell me everything.'

He listened to their account in silence, though there was not much to be told. Once they had done, he stood in thought for some time, though Margot could not guess at what was running through his mind.

'She is gone away on a journey, perhaps,' he ventured after a while.

This was absurd, and he must know it. The nearest town was many miles away; such an expedition had to be meticulously planned. 'The stage does not call at Argantel for two more days, Seigneur,' Margot reminded him. 'And the last coach was three days ago.'

The faint hope died in his eyes, and his lips tightened grimly. 'Sylvie,' he called, scarcely raising his deep voice at all.

Margot had not realised that Sylvaine was present, so quiet had she been. Her quick step was heard from the shop floor, and one slim brown hand appeared betwixt the dangling wooden beads that made up the dividing curtain. She stepped through, making the beads sing in a chorus of clicks and clatters, but the smile she directed at her father swiftly died. 'What is the matter?' she said.

Sylph-like Sylvie was as short as her father was tall, though he never looked down upon her with any condescension. Even now, in all his concern for Oriane, the soft look of approval and affection warmed his gaze, and a swift, unbidden thought flickered through Margot's mind: had her own father ever looked upon her in that way, when he had lived?

'Oriane is not to be found,' said Seigneur Chanteraine very softly.

Sylvaine went still. 'She has been searched for?'

'To some degree. A proper search must be undertaken.'

Sylvaine touched one hand to the wispy halo of heathery-purple hair which framed her delicate face, and her gaze turned distant. Where did her thoughts go? Margot watched as something unidentifiable passed behind Sylvie's eyes, and then she came back to them. "I will see to it,' she said.

Sylvie was a marvel of efficiency, always. To her, Margot gave all the credit for the clever arrangements at the emporium; not a single thing was ever mislaid or out of place, no matter how small or insignificant. Under her direction, all of the emporium's neighbours were roused to the hunt for Oriane, and the search proceeded apace.

But she was not found. Not with her mother, who was growing elderly and often needed the care of a loving daughter; not at any of the houses that shared a street with her little cottage; not with the winemakers, not at the baths, and not seated beneath her favourite lemon tree that stood on the edge of the town square. She had not been seen all day, not at the baker's or the greengrocer's or the tailor's; no glimpse had been caught of her, not anywhere.

Margot was released to her home some hours later, when the Gloaming gave way at last to the deeper darkness of night. So weary was she that she could scarce put one foot in front of the other, but she had not had the heart to request anybody's assistance. What carriages, ponies and mules were available had been pressed into service; beasts and their owners were still engaged in the search for Oriane.

But Pharamond Chanteraine had given up on the likelihood of finding her, as had Sylvie. Was it only Margot's imagination, or had they felt little real hope of finding her at all? What had been the meaning of Seigneur Chanteraine's long silence, and the odd thoughts drifting behind his daughter's eyes? They had exchanged a long look, back there in the storeroom of the emporium, and many thoughts had gone unspoken aloud.

But for all her sense that they knew a number of things they had not shared, she would have sworn that the news of Oriane's absence had been a surprise to them both, and an unwelcome one. Privately, Margot had hoped that the two would announce some insight, some secret information that only they knew, and which would somehow serve to discover where Oriane had gone.

But they had not. She had left them feeling, to all appearances, as frustrated and concerned as was she herself, and with no other suggestions to offer.

It was only later that night, alone in her cramped but beloved little house, and comfortably ensconced in her cool stone parlour with a plate of oat cakes before her, that she remembered an omission: the moth-wing coat. She had not thought to tell Seigneur Chanteraine about it, and Florian had not mentioned it either. The coat, for all its strange beauty, had quite slipped her mind in the urgency of Oriane's absence.

Had she been wrong? She did not see how it could be relevant, but he had said: *Tell me everything.* Did that not suggest that anything could be important? She made up her mind to see the Chanteraines again upon the morrow, as soon as she could be spared from Landricourt, and then she would bear them her forgotten snippet of news.

CHAPTER THREE

Margot rose very early the following morning, as was her wont in the summer. The moment the first glimmers of dawn peeped through the chinks in her shutters, she was awake and swift to rise. A chunk of Seigneur Morel's seed bread — grown a little stale, but flavoursome enough — refreshed her for the day's labours, taken with a glass of marjoram tea. Thus fortified, and dressed in one of the simple brown cotton skirts she so much preferred, Margot ventured out to greet the morning.

Dawn seemed all the more a miracle in the wake of the Gloaming, and Margot savoured every moment of it as she walked into the meadows on the edge of Argantel. Her ultimate destination was, of course, Landricourt, but she had some of her own business to conduct before she took up her duties. Humming a low tune under her breath, she set to work harvesting some portion of the wild thyme, dandelion and clover that grew in clusters among the grasses. It was harder to be at peace on such a morning as this; her serenity was more the product of determined labour than natural ease. Her thoughts *would* keep turning towards poor vanished Oriane, no matter how hard she tried to focus upon the fresh batch of soap she would soon prepare, or the chamomile cream she might venture upon making.

A wander through the wilds could not but help. Margot had always found it soothing to be out in the meadows; when she was a sprout of a child, always coming in late with her hair wind-wild and her feet crusted with fresh earth, her mother had joked that she was a wildling herself. She resembled something woods-wrought, to be sure: her skin was brown as a nut, her unruly hair shaded russet and gold like oak leaves in autumn.

Time passed, and the herbs in Margot's basket grew into satisfying piles. She would have much to occupy herself with in the twilit evenings to come, and perhaps the Chanteraines would take the new chamomile cream for the emporium, once it was complete. She passed from grassy hollows to burgeoning slopes in a half-daze, her churning thoughts lulled into serenity by the peace and abundance of the early morning.

But as she drew nearer to Landricourt, a glimpse of something untoward caught her eye: a flash of colour, something moving nearby. Another person, she thought; but that person was fleeing from her, had secreted themselves behind one of the ancient oaks that grew in the grounds of the grand old house. Margot stopped, and stared hard, but those huge, whorled trunks were more than equal to the concealment of a single person — if a person it had been. Perhaps it had only been a bird, exaggerated in

Margot's mind to much greater proportions.

She paused a moment longer, undecided. The hour grew late, and Landricourt loomed upon the horizon, beckoning her to her day's duties. She had gone through her scant stock of spare hours and had no more left to her; and yet... thoughts of Oriane intruded, scattering her peace. It could not be Oriane, could it? No, why should it be? For nothing reasonable could possess her friend and fellow winemaker to flit from tree to tree in so odd a fashion, concealing herself even from those who were familiar to her.

Nonetheless, Margot could not turn away. Her feet moved almost of their own volition, and she approached the tree, calling doubtfully, 'Oriane?'

There came no reply, and when Margot had traversed the cool shade cast by the wide-spread branches and stepped over the knotted roots that protruded through the earth, a quick step took her behind the trunk and revealed — nothing. No one was there.

'A bird,' she sighed. 'Fool that I am, for what business could Oriane have here?'

Despite her logic, a mild sense of unease prickled at the back of her mind as she turned her face toward Landricourt and trudged on into the growing heat of the morning, the sun's heat already baking the grasses beneath her bare feet. She could not shake the feeling that the flutter of colour had not been a bird, or any animal at all. But if she was right and someone had, briefly, lingered there, where could they have gone, without her noticing their flight? And why had they hidden from her at all?

She was within a few minutes of reaching

Landricourt when the stillness of the morning was split by a great shout. 'Ho, Margot!' came the familiar voice, and Margot turned to find Florian in rapid pursuit of her, his ruffled hair flying like a flag in the breeze.

'Good morning, Florian,' she said, unable to suppress the frown that sprang to her brow.

Florian paused to make her his customary, hasty bow, and smiled at her. 'I hope that doubtful demeanour does not mean that you're unhappy to see me.'

'No, only puzzled. What brings you here so early?'

'My employer has dispatched me to assist you at Landricourt today.'

This was no explanation at all, and Margot did not dignify it with a response. They required no help, which Seigneur Chanteraine must know. And if they did, they would not dragoon his shop boy into bearing them assistance. She raised her brows in mute scepticism, and waited.

Abashed, Florian gave a slight cough and looked at the floor. 'I believe he is concerned for the well-being of the rest of the winemakers, considering the continued absence of Oriane.'

This surprised Margot more than she cared to show. 'Why, does he imagine that more of us may vanish into the wind?'

'He did not choose to share all his thoughts with me, but I think he does.'

Margot felt torn between a stirring of alarm at this idea, and a bubbling of amusement at the prospect of Florian Talleyrand's being sent to protect them from an unknown and unquantifiable threat. Laughter won. 'And how are you to help us, should we be in some danger?'

She regretted her words at once, for though he tried his best to conceal it, Florian was obviously cast down. 'Why, I shall beat off all danger with my bare hands!' he said with some bravado, and tried to make himself taller.

Margot doubted very much that the master of the emporium had sent his youthful employee with any idea as to his defending the winemakers from vanishment. Florian was more likely dispatched to serve as messenger, should anything go amiss — or, more likely, should Oriane reappear. But she said none of this, for he clearly cherished the vision of himself as noble protector, and sent by so august a person as Pharamond Chanteraine himself. So she smiled upon him, and turned her steps once more towards the house. 'We will put you to work, I warn you,' she said as they turned into the courtyard of the house. 'We will feel Oriane's lack today, and Maewen will not hesitate to make use of you.'

'I am ready to work, as always.'

Maewen herself met them as they came into the great hall, her face creased with concern. 'Oriane?' she said.

'No word,' murmured Margot. 'She has not arrived this morning either, I take it?'

Maewen sighed and shook her head, her gaze alighting upon Florian.

He recognised his cue at once, and swept her one of his neater bows. 'Madame Brionnet, I am sent with Seigneur Chanteraine's compliments.'

'For what purpose? Does he require more of the rosewater? I had thought two bottles would be enough.'

'More than, ma'am. I am here—'

'—to help us,' interrupted Margot. 'In the absence of Oriane.' Judging from the worry Maewen was striving, unsuccessfully, to hide, her morning was not to be brightened by the suggestion that Chanteraine feared for her safety, and that of her fellow winemakers.

'How kind of your master,' said Maewen, her face brightening. 'We will be sure to thank him by way of some suitable gift. A taste of the new wine, perhaps? Come, Florian, I will show you where you are to work. Margot, put those in the cellar,' — she indicated Margot's overflowing basket of herbs with a nod — 'and it is gathering for you this morning, if you please. I declare, the rosehips have grown at double their usual rate. What a night it has been! The Gloaming has been kind to us, at least.'

Florian wandered away after Maewen, casting Margot a brief, ironical look on his way out. Margot was amused herself, for all Maewen's abundance of gratitude was directed at Pharamond Chanteraine's generosity rather than at Florian's obedience, when the labour of the gesture would be all performed by the latter.

She had not needed Maewen's information and the instruction came as no surprise, for a glance was enough: the tangled thicket of thorny vines was as heavily burdened by rosehips as it had been yesterday morning, if not more so. It was as though she had not spent some eight or nine hours yesterday collecting rose-berries from those same clambering brambles; indeed, they looked as though they had never been harvested at all. Everywhere she looked, she saw an abundance of plump, pale seed heads, and while the sight had its beauties, to *her* it spoke of aching shoulders and a pain in her lower back, not to mention fingers striped with thorn-scratches.

Never mind it, she told herself sternly, for while her role at Landricourt was wearying and not handsomely paid, it had ample compensations in one form or another.

Margot went to store the first harvest of the day in the cellars as Maewen had directed, and, collecting a pair of trugs on her way back up the stairs, she fell to the second with as much goodwill as she could muster.

The morning passed swiftly enough, and the day wore into afternoon. Margot spent those hours clambering up and down her step-ladder, moving from the vaulted stone hall into the decayed elegance of the dining room, the first and second parlours, and beyond, filling trug after trug with rosehips gleaned from the twisting vines that covered the walls, the ceiling and in some places, parts of the floor. When the sun was at its highest she paused to devour the sweet rolls she had brought with her. Cloudy and soft, lavishly buttered, these were stuffed with the tiny, jewel-like bilberries that grew abundantly among the scattered copses of Vale Argantel, and especially within the tangled forests that crowded the higher slopes. Adelaide arrived just as Margot was licking the butter from her fingertips, her usual smile in place, though there lurked a shadow behind her eyes; she and Oriane had always been particular friends. She wore a blue scarf over her dark hair, keeping the heavy strands out of her face, and blue gems sparked in her ears. She had vanity, Adelaide, but with good reason, for Madame Quincy was generally described as the handsomest woman in the valley, and few would disagree.

'Maewen has ordered double of the honey today,' said Adelaide by way of greeting, setting down a tray clustered with glass jugs and capacious cups. 'And the elderflower.'

Here were treats indeed, for the eldest winemaker was usually sparing with her famed elderflower cordial, and the honey in question was gleaned from the bees in her own, flower-drowned garden. Margot would have given much to know what precisely went into the making of both, for no honey had ever tasted sweeter or more delicious, and no cordial was more refreshing after a morning's labours in the heat.

Whether Maewen was trying to distract the winemakers from Oriane's absence or comfort them under it, Margot could not surmise.

She accepted a large portion of the cordial from Adelaide, watching with relish as the other lady stirred a healthy dollop of honey into the glass, and tried to drink it sparingly. In this, she failed.

Adelaide smiled, and refilled the glass. But the smile soon faded, and she hesitated, on the point of speech.

Margot thought she would raise the subject of Oriane, but instead she said: 'You were the first to arrive, Margot, were you not? This morning. Save only for Maewen, of course.'

'I believe so,' Margot agreed cautiously. 'I did not see or hear anybody else, when I came in.'

Adelaide nodded, but said nothing else, seeming unwilling to speak.

'Why do you ask?' Margot prompted her.

'Did you… happen to see anything unusual, as you approached the house?'

Surprised, Margot said at once: 'I… thought I did, but it turned out to be nothing. A bird darting behind a tree, I think.'

Adelaide's eyes brightened, and she clutched at this meagre offering with, Margot thought, unwonted enthusiasm. 'I had the same experience! Margot, I am persuaded it was not a bird. I am sure there was someone there, only when I went to look, she had faded into the wind.'

'She?'

'I think there was a woman there, for I am sure I saw the flicker of rose-red skirts.'

Rose-red. The words sparked a feeling of recognition in Margot, for she would have used similar words to describe her own brief glimpse of colour. 'But how could she fade into the wind?' she asked.

'I do not know, but I think… I wonder if perhaps it was Oriane? She had a skirt of such a colour, once.'

'Did she?' Margot had not known, and this snippet of information briefly influenced her. But she decided against the idea, and shook her head. 'It cannot be, can it? What would she be doing, darting about the place like a stranger, hiding herself from us?'

'Perhaps something has gone amiss with her,' suggested Adelaide.

'Such as what, that could inspire such peculiar behaviour?'

Adelaide had no answer to give, and no further arguments to offer in support of her theory. Watching the hope fade from her face, Margot felt a brute, to have crushed her tenuous belief in her friend's nearness; but her conviction did not waver. It could not be Oriane.

But, then, who was it? For if Adelaide had seen something out of place this morning, and had, like Margot, been convinced of its being some other person, then Margot was more willing to entertain the real possibility that a stranger wandered the grounds of Landricourt. A stranger who did not wish to be seen.

Her cordial finished, she set her glass back upon Adelaide's tray. 'Where did you see this woman?' she enquired.

Adelaide gestured with one slender hand: away behind the house, far from where Margot had been wandering that morning. 'Betwixt the oaks there. But I have searched them all, Margot, and there is no one now. I have been watching all morning, too, as I could, and have not seen her return.'

Margot waved her upon her way, off to visit and refresh the rest of the winemakers for their afternoon's labours. For herself, she set aside her own work for a few minutes more, and went in search of Florian.

Florian had no information to offer, but he promised to be upon the watch for any further glimpses of a woman with rose-red skirts. With this Margot had to be satisfied, for the rosehips would not wait upon her convenience; several of her fellows were hard at work in the vast, vaulted cellar rooms below the house, crushing and filtering the rosehips she and Adelaide and Florian gathered and beginning the process of transforming them into wine. She could not spare the hour or more it would take to conduct a thorough search of the grounds. She resolved to take up the search later in the afternoon, when the onset of the twilight declared an end to the labours of the day. And she would take Florian with her.

As it happened, however, she did not have to wait nearly so long for an answer to the mystery.

For reasons best known to themselves, the majority of the rose-brambles had mostly colonised only the great dining room, the parlours, the drawing room and the bedchambers, leaving such spaces as the kitchens, the long gallery and the grand hall largely unexplored. Accordingly, Margot's daily round ran from the dining room around and up through the bedchambers, and she paused only briefly to look in upon the rest of the house.

But today was different. Upon reaching the long gallery, she noticed two unusual things almost at once.

For the first: the roses had changed their minds about the gallery. Hitherto, they had only peeped tentatively into it from a far, upper corner, sending forth but few leafy tendrils to mingle with the soft, green-daubed murals arrayed across the walls. But somewhere in between Margot's last visit and today — had it been only yesterday, that she had last looked in? — the entirety of the far wall was awash with a thicket of glossy rose leaves and thorny, tangled vines. Unlike those in the rest of the house, whose petals were falling as they formed their plump rosehips, these were in full bloom; there must be hundreds of flowers, Margot thought dazedly, and their scent thickened the air with a heavy floral pungency. Nor was their growth haphazard, to her further astonishment. The spaces upon the walls where portraits had once hung — rectangular patches, brighter with colour than the more faded paint around them — had been left untouched, while twining ropes of thorn-clad stalks had snaked and twisted and coiled unhindered over the rest of the wall, following the shapes of the elegant curlicues and ornately coiling leaves that lay, painted and inert, beneath them. The effect was a new, curiously flourishing mural worked in living greenery, splashed everywhere about with the bright-white petals in their fragrant clusters.

The roses were reaching for the adjacent wall; Margot fancied she could almost *see* them growing as she watched. A particularly enterprising tendril was reaching for the ears of a great white horse painted between two windows, the beast rearing in elegant indignation. It now wore a crown of budding roses.

The second point of interest was this: that the grandly oversized chair lingering in solitary splendour at the distant end was now occupied.

Margot had always secretly adored that chair. It was so stupendously overdone: more than big enough to seat two side-by-side, its back rose to a towering height, its arms too high to rest comfortably upon. It more nearly resembled a throne than a chair, especially situated as it was amidst such grandeur. And while the chair was as decayed as the gallery itself, its cream silk upholstery tattered and frayed and its frame riddled with the scars of woodworm, it had endured. Margot admired that in a chair.

It made a strange, but strangely fitting, seat for the woman who now sat enthroned upon it, her legs crossed beneath the layered, rose-red silks of her skirts. Her bodice was of crimson velvet, and a shawl as light and delicate as tangled spider's webs hung over her thin shoulders. One toe peeped out from beneath the vivid silks, revealing the tip of a silvery silken slipper. The shoe was stained with rosy colours, as though she had been dancing through a thick carpet of rose petals. Her thin, white fingers were held up before her, for between them a web every bit as ethereal and tangled as her shawl was strung in glittering strands, anointed here and there with diamond-bright droplets of dew. She was absorbed in the contemplation of her web, so much so that she did not appear to notice Margot's entrance at all. Her fine-featured face was as white as the roses around her, the eyes so intent upon her work an eerily bright green against such pallor. Amber-winged moths had settled in the wispy mass of her pale, gold-spun hair; Margot thought them fanciful ornaments, until startled by the flicker of a wing into a realisation that they were quite real.

Surprised beyond all power of speech, Margot stood in thunderstruck silence for some moments, watching the singular woman with something like awe. Her amazement only grew when, with a delicate flicker of her fingers, the woman set the fragile strands of her web shivering; the dewdrops twinkled, moon-bright, and — Margot did not think it was her imagination — the creeping tendrils of the rose-thicket crept a little farther onward, slowly unfurling polished green leaves at their lady's command.

It occurred to Margot that the ragged throne was the source of the thicket, the central point from which all vines fanned outwards. Who was this woman, that the roses stretched and grew and blossomed at her whim?

Margot realised, with a jolt, that those searing green eyes had focused upon her; she was herself observed. She swallowed a sudden flutter of fear — what was she to be afraid of? No move had this visitor made to harm her, or any of the winemakers, and there had been opportunity enough — and spoke. 'Who are you?'

Those green eyes flickered. 'They call me Rozebaiel,' said the woman, and the web shivered under the soft exhalation of her breath. She added, 'Sometimes,' in a softer tone, scarcely more than a whisper. Then her emerald gaze sharpened upon Margot, and she said in a challenging way: 'And who are *you*? This is not my Landricourt. What have you done with it?' The name, *Landricourt*, Margot recognised, though Rozebaiel had not spoken it in the usual way. There came an unusual inflection; the syllables formed more of a *Laendricourt*.

'I—' Margot stopped, unsure what to say, for of course it was Landricourt. What else could it be supposed to be? 'I am Margot de Courcey,' she offered, resolving to let the other matter slide. 'I am a winemaker here.'

'Wine?' said Rozebaiel sharply, and looked wildly about, as though expecting to see the evidence of it materialise at any moment. 'You make the amberwyne *here*?'

'The... the amberwine?' repeated Margot, nonplussed. 'I do not think I ever heard it called such—'

As she spoke, Rozebaiel dropped her tangled web of gossamer strands — which vanished, smoke-like, into the air — and snatched the head from a drowsing rose peeping over her left shoulder. This she thrust at Margot, interrupting her. '*These*,' she said forcefully, though not quite in anger. 'What are they!'

'R-roses,' said Margot, aware as she spoke that the obvious answer was not the one sought, but unable to give any other.

Rozebaiel tenderly stroked the pallid petals of the rose she held, then tossed it negligently onto the floor. It lay there, three petals fallen onto the rotting floorboards and the rest already wilting.

Margot found her voice. 'Forgive me,' she said, for it never hurt to be polite, however peculiar the circumstances. 'How came you to be here?'

Anger — if that was what it was — drained out of Rozebaiel's delicate face and her extraordinary eyes grew large with distress. 'I do not know, but I should very much like to go back. At *once*.'

'Back to where? Where is it that you are from?'

'Laendricourt.'

'But *this* is Landricourt.'

'Whatever it may be, it is not *my* Laendricourt! It is some semblance only, an echo, and *what* an echo! How can you have let it fall into ruin?' Rozebaiel looked at Margot with such reproach that she felt shamed, as though she was personally responsible for the house's state. But that was nonsense. It must have been well on its way to ruin by the time Margot was born.

'It *is* a great shame,' she agreed, staring in familiar sadness at the faded walls; the gaping patch in the middle of the floor where the boards had fallen through; the softly glowing pools of light that filtered through the holes in the ceiling. 'I have often wondered who owns it, how they can have permitted—'

'Owns it?' interrupted Rozebaiel. 'No one can own Laendricourt.'

Margot blinked. 'Well, then of course it is a ruin.'

Rozebaiel's head tilted. 'How so?'

'Why, if it is owned by no one then nobody is responsible for its maintenance.'

'All are responsible,' said Rozebaiel.

The import of Rozebaiel's earlier words struck Margot all at once, and she gasped. 'What do you mean, you do not know how you came to be here?'

'I mean,' said Rozebaiel slowly, 'that a day ago and a half I was *there*, and now I am *here*.'

'A day and a half! Why, that is just when Oriane disappeared — or it may be, she has not been seen since. I wonder—'

There was no point in finishing the sentence, for at mention of the word *disappeared,* Rozebaiel darted out of her chair and, with a quick, fierce look at Margot, she turned in a swirl of ethereal shawl and flyaway hair and vanished at a run through the far door.

By the time Margot reached the door, there was no further sign of Rozebaiel; the long corridor stretching beyond was empty in both directions.

Margot turned back into the gallery, nonplussed. Lying on the vacated chair was a thin ribbon of cloth, a gauzy thing as cloudy-light as Rozebaiel's shawl, and as pale as the roses in the midst of which she had sat enthroned. Margot picked it up, handling it with care, for the cloth was so delicate she feared she might break it. It glistened as if with dew, like the web Rozebaiel had been weaving among her fingers; but when Margot touched it, she found the droplets were not water. They had no substance to them at all.

She would go to Florian, she decided, and show him this thing, in proof of a tale that might otherwise seem implausibly wild. But as she turned to leave, she noticed something else curious. Above the threadbare throne, nestled so deep within a tangle of leaves that Margot had almost missed it, was a single blossom out of place among the its brethren; for while the petals that ringed the outer edge of the flower were of the customary pallid, moon-pale hue, its heart flushed a deep, harvest gold.

Margot had not much time to wonder at this change, for as she gazed upon the two-toned rose, the great clock chimes began to strike across the Vale; the Gloaming was coming in.

PART TWO

FLORIAN

CHAPTER ONE

Florian had not been entirely honest with Margot. *Seigneur Chanteraine did not choose to share all his thoughts with me,* he had told her, which was undoubtedly true as far as it went. But the enigmatic master of the emporium had shared one or two more musings with his employee than Florian had imparted to Margot.

Chanteraine had been troubled that morning, and visibly so, which was unlike him; so adept was he at maintaining a consistently calm, composed demeanour, Florian was used to having to guess at his master's true feelings. But today was different.

Florian always arrived at the emporium very early. By the time the pink light of sunrise spilled across the skies, he was already at work: in the storeroom taking stock of the shop's supplies, or packing the first orders of the day for later delivery. But this morning, he had arrived to find Chanteraine already there; and if much was to be construed from the drawn look about the master's face, he had been there all night.

'Florian,' he'd said in his grave way, 'I have a different duty for you today.'

'I am at your service, sir, as always,' Florian had dutifully replied.

'There is something gone awry at Landricourt, I fear,' said the master of the emporium, and held up a hand to forestall the questions which threatened to tumble from Florian's lips. 'Do not ask me the nature of the disturbance, for I cannot tell you. I only know that it must be at Landricourt... it *must*.' This last was spoken in a lower tone, as though Chanteraine's mind had wandered from Florian and he spoke more to himself than to his shop boy; the distant look in his wintry-blue eyes rather reinforced this impression.

'Sir?' prompted Florian, when some moments passed in silence.

Pharamond Chanteraine recalled himself from wherever it was that he had gone, and contrived to focus upon the countenance of his shop boy. 'Yes. You must find out the nature of the disturbance. You will find Madame Brionnet amenable to your presence, though you may wish to conceal your investigations from the winemakers. I would not like for them to be any more alarmed than they are already.'

By the disappearance of Oriane, Florian supplied, finishing the sentence in his own mind, even if his master could not say the words.

And so Florian had found himself dispatched to Landricourt forthwith. On the way there he saw Margot, and paused a moment to admire the picture that she made: her laden basket swinging from one brown arm, holding her skirts out of the way of her feet as she wandered the brightening meadows. She looked so at peace at that hour, alone among the dawn-kissed beauty of the vale, a faint breeze stirring the russet tangle of her hair. He had not wanted to intrude, but she had seen him, and fallen to questioning. His lie she had seen through with embarrassing ease, and he had tried to give her a better, fuller answer.

47

But Chanteraine had said: *I need for you to act secretly for me in this, Florian. I would not like it known that I am minded to interfere in the matter of Landricourt.*

This reticence did not make sense to Florian, for Chanteraine's long friendship with Oriane was widely known, and his deeper fondness for her popularly suspected. But in this, as in all things, Florian had acquiesced, though it chafed him to have to keep secrets from Margot.

It was to his mingled relief and regret that they were parted the moment they stepped into the cool stone hall at Landricourt, for she went away at once to store her harvest, and begin afresh, and he was whisked straight down into the cellars by Madame Brionnet, and given a trug like Margot's. 'It is so kind of you to help us in the absence of Oriane,' she said, loudly enough; and then more quietly, too low to be overheard, 'And kinder still to help us under these strangest of circumstances. Mr. Chanteraine has spoken to you of…?'

Florian waited, but she did not finish the sentence. 'Yes,' he said, somewhat uncertainly. 'I am to search the house for anything… untoward.' It occurred to him as he said it that his presence there was not much justified. If Madame Brionnet wanted the house searched, why should she not do it herself? She spent all day at Landricourt, every day, and had ample opportunity to search all day today if she so chose. And more successfully, too, for she knew the house far better than he — far better, in all probability, than anybody.

He said some of this, as respectfully as he could, but he did not receive the satisfaction of much response. Madame Brionnet said something about "fresh eyes", and briskly moved on to the matter of his ostensible duties. 'You will join the gathering team today, though Margot has the hips well in hand, so it is to be the petals for you. There will not be so many of those left now, so it is a light duty. Just the fresh ones, please. Take the plump ones, the pale velvet ones. Any that are withered or discoloured, you may leave. Empty your trug in the collecting room: down the cellar stairs, and the third door on the left. Have you any questions?'

Florian had a great many, but considering the fate of his earlier enquiries he did not expect that any of them would be answered. So he kept his eyes on the floor, shook his head, and went away with his trug with as good grace as he could manage. He did not much enjoy the sensation of being caught in a web of little mysteries stretching from the Chanteraines at the emporium, to Oriane and Madame Brionnet and Landricourt in general. At least Margot did not seem to be harbouring secrets.

Much of his morning passed thereafter in a haze of activity, though without producing anything of particular note. All across the great, sprawling manor of Landricourt he wandered, first through the kitchens and scullery and the pantries; the boot-room and the cloak-room, the still-rooms, old butler's pantry and what had once been the housekeeper's room. He rambled afterwards through the parlours and the drawing-rooms, the morning-room and dining chambers, the grand hall, an amber-clad salon and the long gallery. He vigorously poked his nose into every corner of every room, dutiful in the performance of this nosiest of duties; and when anybody happened to pass by the room in which he was hard at labour, their footsteps ringing helpfully upon the bared wood or stone tiles of the adjoining corridors, he fell to harvesting rose-petals as tenderly as he could, taking great care not to crush the delicate things.

He met Margot once, halfway up her weathered step-ladder in the far corner of the ballroom. She hailed him at once, abandoning her efforts to strip the nearby vines of their fruits, and hastily clambered down the steps again. Resisting the temptation to rush there and hold the ladder — to wait below, in case she should happen to miss her step and fall — he approached at a more reasonable pace, ready to dart forward had she need. But though she was undoubtedly in a state of some excitement, she was as sure-footed as a goat, and whisked her way down to the ground again without wavering one whit. 'I did not tell you before,' she said, her tawny eyes alight; he experienced a brief hope that their sparkling expression owed something to his appearance, but was soon forced to abandon any such sentimental ideas. Her attention was all for her tale. 'This morning, shortly before I met you on the way, I thought I saw something — a person, maybe a woman, wearing red. I thought little of it, but Adelaide has just said that she has seen something the same. Have you noticed anything like that, Florian? Adelaide thinks it is Oriane, but I cannot agree with her.'

Florian did not agree with Adelaide either. In fact, he thought he had rarely heard so addle-brained a notion. But the news interested him, for was this not exactly the kind of thing he had been instructed to watch for? He pressed Margot for more detail, and was disappointed that she could provide little more — only that Adelaide had described the woman's garb as "rose-red" — forgetting perhaps, in her use of common parlance, that roses of that colour had not been seen in Argantel in many years.

'I will watch for this lady,' Florian readily agreed.

'And do tell me of it, should you chance to see her!' requested Margot.

He agreed to this, too, not at all sorry to have a reason to come in search of her again — supposing he had the luck to run into the mysterious lady in the rose-red gown, of course. Did he flatter himself that Margot seemed reluctant to part with him, as he turned away? No — she was only enjoying the interlude his presence provided, revelling in having an excuse to pause her labours for a little while.

Florian took himself off, resolving on searching the ballroom when Margot had finished with it.

Luncheon came, courtesy of one of the winemakers. She did not offer her name, and Florian felt indisposed for conversation. So many hours labouring in the heat had left him in no fit state for company; his cotton shirt clung to his back, soaked through with sweat, and he knew that his face shone with it. His hair… he did not want to imagine what had become of his hair. He dispatched his ration of thick seeded bread, strong cheese and honey cordial with gusto, and, feeling much refreshed, he began anew rather higher up in the house than he had ever ventured before. He climbed and climbed up the rickety, rowan-wood staircase that spiralled a tight path up into the south-western tower, following a trail of rose-blooms that seemed especially replete with pale, perfect petals. So absorbed was he in the gathering of these, and in peeping through the tapestry of leaves for signs of anything hidden behind, that he did not notice the rose-red woman until she spoke to him.

'Why do you strip the flowers of their gowns?' she said to him, a voice of unusually low registers winding through the sun-blasted air like a trickle of treacle.

He fumbled his trug in his surprise; almost dropped it; saved it at last, though a flurry of velvet petals were cast overboard and sailed, fluttering, onto the dust-thick steps beneath his feet. He had to climb the rest of them before he saw who addressed him, hoping all the while that it was the very lady he sought; *one* step, *two, three*, and he came out into a little turret chamber, round-walled and painted white, the high vault of its ceiling liberally hung with ancient cobwebs. The sun shone, full and fierce, through the long windows that lit the walls in every direction, though the light was much dimmed by the tangle of rose-vines; they had crept through the spaces left by missing panes of glass and run rampant thereafter, claiming most of the walls and half the floor as their own. Only the ceiling was largely untouched, as though the flowers had come to some agreement with the spiders of Landricourt, and left their lofty territory largely untouched.

An arbour had formed among some of these vines, a nook just large enough to accommodate one woman, provided she were not so very tall. And she was not by any means tall, the woman in rose-red. She sat among the roses as though upon a pretty swing, her hands wound about with leafy tendrils and roses blooming at her feet. Her skirts fell in rosy layers all about her, and the rest of her dress was all of velvet.

Her wide-set eyes were almost painfully bright green, sunk deep in a pale face flecked with freckles like spatters of gold paint. Her hair was like a tangle of corn silk.

Florian did not know what to say. He gaped at this vision, words forming in his thoughts only to vanish like morning mist when he groped after them.

'It is very rude,' added rose-red, and Florian wondered distantly whether she was referring to his harvesting of the petals, or to his silent gawping.

He flushed and averted his eyes, setting his trug down carefully upon the floor. Delicate tendrils curled up and over the edge of the basket at once, as though claiming it for their own; Florian half expected to see it sail away, borne on a tide of rose-leaves, though thankfully it did not.

'I-I must, ma'am,' he offered. 'They are to be made into rosewater, and they would only die if they were not gathered up.'

'They would give of themselves readily enough, were you to *ask*,' she said with asperity, and held up one small, long-fingered hand, palm upwards, beneath a particularly fat rose that hovered near to her left ear. 'Shall you please?' she said sweetly, and the rose shook itself, like a dog shaking grass-seed from its coat. A rain of petals floated free and drifted into the cupped palm beneath, to its owner's smug-smiling satisfaction. The trug did move, then, drifting towards the girl in the arbour. When it arrived at her feet, she bent down and let the petals fall into it. 'You must not be rude,' she said to Florian earnestly. 'Should you like it if I took that pretty neckcloth, and without asking?'

'P-pretty...?' Florian owned no "pretty"

neckcloths; his were all of plain cotton, all function and no grace whatsoever. Today's was plain white, and in no state to be admired after the exertions of the day; it had been soaking up his perspiration all morning.

But he could not help casting an involuntary glance at it as he spoke, though he knew very well what it must look like. And there he was brought up short, for his ordinary white neckcloth was nowhere in evidence. Around his neck he now wore a flimsy dream of a thing, all amber-bright, made, at least as far as it *looked*, from the substance of flower petals. Its edges curled into tight scrolls, its surface scattered with a pattern of delicate holes, like lace.

'Th-this is not mine,' said Florian, loathing the way his voice shook as he spoke. It was not merely the peculiarity of everything in this high tower-room that unsettled him, and the odd behaviour of his neckcloth, in changing itself into something else; it was rose-red herself. Her presence filled the room so thoroughly, Florian felt there was scarce room left even for air. He fought to breathe, and only just restrained himself in time from catching at the pretty neckcloth and tugging it looser, and quite ruining it in the process.

'Well! Why would you be wearing it, if it is not yours?' Rose-red's brows snapped together. Was it Florian's imagination, or did the neckcloth tighten about his perspiring neck in the same moment, cutting off the breath he was in the process of drawing?

'A very reasonable question,' he said, rather weakly. How had he come to be wearing it? What had become of his old neckcloth? He could muster no other response, for he had no answers to give. He wanted to take the lovely thing off at once, and give it to *her*, for it was clearly the sort of thing better suited to a woman dressed like a flower and with moths in her hair. But she gave him a narrow-eyed look, as though she had anticipated his intention and disapproved heartily of the idea.

Florian decided he was tired of feeling wrong-footed and uncertain, and mustered himself to go on the attack. 'Forgive me, ma'am,' he said — for however much he might wish to assert himself, it would never do to be impolite. 'But who are you, and how did you come to be here?'

'I do not know how I came here,' she said, ignoring the first of Florian's questions entirely. She said it in tones of great dissatisfaction tinged with petulance, and underneath all that there lingered a trace of distress. 'What have you done to the Wind's Own Tower? Where are the looms, and the great glass jars?' She glared about herself as if greatly upset by everything that she saw — or perhaps, considering her words, by everything she was not seeing.

'I do not know what you speak of,' said Florian. 'There has never been anything of that kind here, not for as long as I can remember. No one has ever spoken of anything like that, or — or used such a peculiar name! This is the southwest tower, if it is ever given a name at all, and no one ever comes here.'

'*You* are here,' she said silkily.

'Only to collect the rose-petals, and I shall soon have done with that, and go away again.'

'And why do you take them away?'

'They are to be made into perfume-water.' Florian spoke rather shortly, feeling tired of the endless questions when she had been so little inclined to answer his own.

He need not have taken the trouble of trying to discourage her, for she asked only one last question: 'Ah!' said she. 'Where do you take them, petal-gatherer?'

'Down into the cellars, to the stillrooms there,' he replied, and upon these brief words, she leapt out of her little arbour of leaves and ran lightly away down the spiralling stairs.

'Ma'am?' he called. 'You have left something behind.' But she did not hear him, or perhaps she did but did not choose to return. Florian picked up the abandoned object with care, and found it to be a tiny phial, oddly shaped and too lightweight for glass, and strung upon a short length of silvery chain. Within there swirled something like coiled mist, rose-tinted like the woman who had lost it.

If he had seen her once he would, in all likelihood, see her again, thought Florian. He would go down to the cellars directly and see if she had gone to the stillrooms, and return the curious trinket at once.

But when he arrived in the blissfully cool cellars and went from stillroom to stillroom — and then from storeroom to storeroom, and through every other chamber after that — he found no trace of rose-red. No one else had seen her, either, he soon found.

No one, that is, except for Margot. The next time he saw her, she was deep in the greenery infesting the jade parlour (so called for the jade-coloured paintings of some strange, undersea scene that spanned its expansive ceiling). She was half-hidden among the roses, and growing weary now; she moved with the care and slowness of a woman with an aching back, and a rapidly diminishing enthusiasm for her tasks.

'Margot,' he softly called, unwilling to startle her again by a too-rapid approach.

She turned at once, and came forward to meet him with an eager step. But as he opened his mouth to tell her that he had found the red-skirted woman, she forestalled him by saying, 'What do you think, Florian? I have seen her! Spoken to her, even! Her name is Rozebaiel — the woman in red, I mean — and she...' She stopped, and looked him over. 'Where did you get that neckcloth?' she said.

'Rozebaiel,' he replied. 'Or so I assume, for it appeared around my neck while I was up in the southwest tower, and she was there. Though I do not know what has become of my old one.' He showed her the mist-trinket, too, and received a glimpse in return of a similar acquisition of hers: a length of cloudy, gauzy ribbon all a-twinkle.

'The moth-wing coat,' said Florian.

Margot's eyes grew wide and round. 'I had half-forgotten it, Florian, but you are right. It is of a piece with these things, is it not? I wonder where—' she stopped again, and interrupted herself; Florian gathered that her mind was spinning so fast she could hardly keep up with herself. 'The Chanteraines must know what to make of them, if anybody does. Are they not a little like the curiosities Pharamond sells at the emporium?'

'They're far stranger,' said Florian. 'But a little like.'

Margot immediately gave her ribbon into his possession. 'We left the coat at Oriane's house, did we not? It must be got back, and taken to the emporium. I wonder we did not think of it before.'

'I will go,' Florian agreed, recognising his cue. He had much to tell Seigneur Chanteraine as it was, for was Rozebaiel's appearance not precisely the kind of thing he had been sent to search for? She was certainly an anomaly, and full strange… He debated whether to tell Madame Brionnet about it first, but decided against; it was for his master to decide how far abroad to spread that tale. 'I shall—'

His next words went unheard, for they were drowned by the sound of the great clock striking its first chime. *One.*

'Odd,' said Margot. 'What can have distracted Adelaide? She has not—'

Two.

'—begun the song.'

Florian waited, expecting to hear the winemaker's evensong beginning at any moment.

Three.

But the song did not come.

And neither did the fourth chime.

The Gloaming, however, *did.* Unfazed by this deviation from the daily rituals, it swept across Argantel in its usual fashion: a great swoop of blanketing night-shadow, muting the summer sun and cutting straight through its fierce heat. In the space of a few breaths, Margot became an indistinct silhouette to Florian's eye, her figure only dimly outlined in the sudden gloom of the parlour.

'What—' said Margot, but she did not finish the sentence.

'Is there a lamp hereabouts?' said Florian, for he had fished out his battered copper pocket-watch; but no matter how fiercely he peered at its glass face, he could not make out the time.

He heard Margot's soft footsteps as she moved, slowly and carefully, to some other part of the room, and came back again. 'I have got a lamp,' she said, 'and I hope you have got a striker.'

He did, by fortune. The lamp was lit, and Margot's face shone suddenly illuminated in its soft, clear light. 'What says your watch?' she whispered.

'Three.' Florian had checked it thrice over, unwilling to believe the story it told. The Gloaming came in at four; it had always done so, and must always do so, for its habits were as regular and predictable as the rising of the sun, or the phases of the moon; when had it ever varied before?

'*Three,*' echoed Margot. 'Are you quite sure?'

Mute, he held up the watch for her to see for herself. She stared at it.

'I think,' she said slowly, 'that you had better see Pharamond, and the sooner the better.'

Florian could not disagree. 'Will you come with me?' was all that he said.

Margot looked as though she wanted to object; her gaze travelled back to the unharvested rosehips, and the half-full trug she had left upon the floor. But the winemakers' day ended when the Gloaming came in; such was always the case, for how they could work effectively when they could hardly see what they were doing? 'I will,' she decided, and picked up her trug. 'Let us deliver these to Maewen,' and she indicated his basket of petals, too, with a nod of her head, 'And we will go.'

CHAPTER TWO

The house of Oriane seemed, somehow, darker and emptier than it had before, and it held an air of stillness, as though its owner had been gone for far longer than a day or two. Florian felt his skin shiver as he and Margot walked into the little kitchen, he holding high the lamp borrowed from the jade parlour at Landricourt. 'Where was it that we found the coat?' he asked Margot.

Margot went straight to the rocking-chair by the hearth. The gauzy garment was still there, its delicate embroidery shining over-bright in the soft lamplight. Margot picked it up, handling it as though it might fall to pieces under the force of a single exhalation — and it looked as though it might. She laid it over one arm, carefully, carefully, and turned back to Florian.

But he was not where she had left him, for he had wandered off to the table in the middle of the room. There in the centre of its simple blue table-cloth stood the glass bottle of pale, golden liquid from Chanteraine's Emporium, and the tiny peacock-coloured book.

'It is a shame Oriane never received those,' said Margot frowningly, 'Though I suppose she is not in need of the elixir, after all.'

Florian did not reply, for his eye had been drawn more to the book than the bottle. He had not looked closely at it before, for his master was always putting some odd thing or another into his hands and dispatching both him and it upon this or that errand. He knew his duty: to deliver, not to pry. But a faint glimmer caught his attention. Though the book's cover was plain — a rich blue silk, unadorned, and with no name or title printed upon it — it did have a length of violet ribbon slipped between its pages. Florian had taken it to be a page marker, and had not given it a second glance. But something glimmered there, the way the moth-wing coat glistered under lamplight.

He picked it up. So tiny, the delicate thing, and lightweight, though it held many pages between its bindings. His master's work, he thought, of a surety; Seigneur Chanteraine had bound books before, often with silken covers like this one.

He opened it, carefully, at the page marked by the length of ribbon. Light glittered, a soft light like distant stars, and he realised it was not ribbon at all — not the satin kind, that might be bought by the yard at Valentin's Haberdashers. It was finely woven, like the moth-wing coat, and embroidered in the same way.

The marked page held no words, only a printed image. It was a painting of Landricourt: the ballroom, he might have said, for the shape and proportions of the room looked the same, and there was the familiar profusion of roses. But this ballroom was not ruined, so why were the roses there? And why were they red and purple and amber, not moon-white? Moreover, its décor was entirely different. The marble floor was no longer pale and serene; it was painted in a wash of colour, jade-green and sage and a soft sky-blue, and several other shades besides. The walls held their usual complement of murals, all vibrant with a freshness their living counterparts no longer displayed. But he did not recognise the images there, half-glimpsed beneath the rose bowers. They were of unfamiliar plants and trees he had never seen, either in life or in paintings, and equally peculiar creatures crouched among the grasses. He thought that there was some sort of glade depicted, lined with trees on one side, but he could not see enough of the mural to be sure; the artist had painted over much of it with roses.

Margot had come up behind him, and stood staring at the print with the same awed silence as he himself. 'Did Mr. Chanteraine paint that?' she asked.

'I don't know. I never saw him paint, but… he is full of talents.'

'And mysteries.'

'Always those, too, yes. I am quite sure that he made the book, but the painting?' Florian shrugged, and carefully turned a page. The next print was also of Landricourt, the jade parlour this time, though this, too, was altered: its walls were painted with soft gold and ivory and pearly-white as well as jade, and a thick mossy carpet covered the floor (was it a carpet indeed, or was it that moss itself had somehow grown from wall to wall?). A low table, perhaps for tea, stood in the centre of the room, though its design was curious: it had five curved, twisting legs, and it appeared to be made from smoky glass. A chaise longue of pearly velvet stood behind it. Roses covered the ceiling and hung from the walls, though these, too, were not silver-pale; they were rich amber and gold and blood-red, like Rozebaiel's skirts.

Page after page he turned, and each held the same thing: paintings of every room in Landricourt, printed in vivid inks, and each decidedly altered from its present composition.

'It is Landricourt as it was,' said Margot. 'Before it was ruined.'

But Florian could not agree. 'Landricourt never looked like this. Have the paintings on the walls all changed, with the passage of time? And though there isn't much furniture left there, none of it looks like *this*.'

Margot frowned. 'But it is Landricourt. Do you not agree?'

'Oh, I agree. But it is some artist's impression of the place, very fanciful. I wonder why Mr. Chanteraine sent it to Oriane.' He went back to the beginning of the book, and found a few more prints showing the grounds at the great house, well-kept instead of a rambling mess, and (perhaps oddly) almost devoid of the roses which colonised the building itself. But some of the plants which grew in these imagined gardens were the same as those of the imagined murals, and the flowers were quite bizarre: trumpets and bells and flutes of soft, curling petals, many the same silver-pale as the roses at the real Landricourt.

'I don't understand it,' he decided at last, and carefully closed the book. 'My master found them somewhere, I dare say, and thinking them a pleasing oddity bound them up for Oriane.'

'I can well imagine that she would like them,' said Margot, and Florian detected a touch of envy in her voice. *She* obviously liked them very well indeed. The winemakers, he supposed, were far more familiar with Landricourt than he; probably they loved the old place as a second home.

He gave her the book. 'We had better not leave these just lying here. Anything might happen to them.'

'You mean, I suppose, that well-meaning souls might come in with many a good intention, and walk out again with moth-wing coats and books and elixirs stuffed into their pockets?'

'Exactly,' said Florian gravely. 'We cannot be too careful with Oriane's things. My master would insist upon it.' And he would, in point of fact, for all that Florian was jesting. These things were clearly important somehow, though Florian could not say why.

Margot tucked the book into a pocket of her dress. 'And the elixir, what of that?'

Florian was, by this time, deeply interested in the elixir. Mr. Chanteraine had called it "restorative", and perhaps that was all it was: a tonic to make her well again, supposing she had been ill. But he had never seen bottles like these in his master's storerooms, or elixirs like that. He picked it up, took out the stopper, and inhaled.

Immediately he passed it under Margot's nose. 'What do you smell?'

'Rose,' she said promptly. 'Rosewater?'

Florian thought of the heavy jars of rosewater he and Margot had so lately hauled down from

Landricourt to the Emporium. Was this what his master had done with all his stock, that he needed more?

Florian took another sniff. 'Rosewater,' he agreed, 'and wine, too, I think. *Your* wine.' He was not often given rosehip wine to drink, but its sweet, autumnal aroma was impossible to mistake.

'A restorative made from rosewater, and rosehip wine?' Margot gazed at the bottle as though it might give up its secrets, if only she were to entreat it hard enough. 'And why, then, is it gold? There must be some other things in there.'

'One way to find out.' Florian tipped up the bottle and took a sip.

'Florian!' Margot protested. 'I cannot think it's right for you to do that.'

Florian ignored this, for how were they ever to find anything out otherwise? 'It tastes of...' he paused, and took a second sip. 'Sunlight and oranges, with a trace of evening mist.'

Margot stared blankly.

'I don't know,' Florian explained, shrugging. 'I can't determine anything else, except maybe for the oranges. That part might be true.'

He blinked, for he thought suddenly of a moonlit arbour in a garden somewhere — at Landricourt, again? The place was ringed with small, ancient trees, boughs swaying in the wind. Where had he seen this place, and how could he have forgotten it? But he blinked again and the thought faded, and there was only Margot looking at him like he was mad.

'Try it,' he said, and offered her the bottle.

She declined. 'I can't think that I would do a better job at guess-the-ingredients than you.'

'You're afraid of what my master would think.'

Margot looked ready to deny it, but decided otherwise. 'All right, yes, I am a little.'

Florian grinned, and tucked the bottle into the crook of his arm. 'He is not so imposing really, once you get to know him.'

'Are you sure?' Margot looked dubious.

'He's a good man.' But Florian could not go so far as to say that the master of the Emporium would *not* be angry, if he knew that they had sampled the elixir concocted for Oriane alone. So he hastily set the subject aside, saying instead, 'Away we go. We had better get to the emporium before the Chanteraines leave.'

Margot gave him one of her suspicious looks, and he knew he would wilt under that gaze if he suffered it for too long. So he strode to the door and held it for the lady, bowing slightly as she passed through it. 'After you, ma'am.'

'Too kind.' Her tone was haughty, but a smile followed, so he knew it was all right.

The lamps were lit at the emporium, so it came as a surprise to Florian to find it empty when he and Margot arrived. He went from room to room, but neither Chanteraine nor his daughter were to be found; not in the storeroom, not on the shop floor, and not in the workshops upstairs. The door to Chanteraine's private chamber was shut, as always; it was the one room Florian was forbidden to enter. He tapped upon the door, but no response came, and no light glimmered around the door.

It was odd of them to go away during opening hours, and leave the shop unattended. But Mr.

Chanteraine had realised that Florian would soon return, no doubt, and consented to be called away.

He'd left Margot kicking her heels in the storeroom. When he clattered his way back down the narrow wooden stairs, he found her eyeing the rows of coloured-glass bottles lined up upon the shelves. 'What is in all these?' she asked, without turning her attention from the bottles.

'Cordials,' said Florian. 'Tinctures, elixirs, assorted refreshing beverages.'

Margot turned to him, her eyes alight, but he could read the question in them without waiting for her to speak. He chose to forestall it. 'Seigneur does not share the recipes, except with Syl— with Demoiselle Chanteraine, of course.' He did not add that he knew where the recipes were to be found. His master kept a book, one he had bound himself in crimson leather. It went everywhere with him, and he referred to it constantly — especially when he was in one of the workshops upstairs, brewing up batches of some cordial or another or fashioning one of the trinkets, jewel-pieces or toys that were so popular with the townspeople. Florian did not doubt that all his recipes were written therein, but he had never had the chance to peek at its contents. He was not sure that he would, if such an opportunity materialised. He was as curious as Margot — probably more so — but to steal such knowledge could not sit well with him.

He'd had hopes, once. He had begun work as the emporium's shop boy years before, at the age of fifteen; the Chanteraines had taken pity on him, for his mother and father were gone and he'd had two younger siblings to provide for. He had dreamed of a future as the Chanteraines' apprentice; perhaps they wanted help with creating the strange and wonderful things that were sold in the shop, and he would be taught to assist. But years had passed, his brother and sister had grown beyond his help, and here he still was: a shop boy, bound to keep counter at his master's need, responsible for the storeroom, and otherwise employed to fetch and carry and make deliveries.

He had buried those disappointments long ago.

'You had better go home, hadn't you? Shall I walk you?' Florian made himself say. He liked seeing Margot here, wandering the storeroom in all her colours, her face alight with wonder and curiosity. He liked that he had been the means of giving her the chance to explore; it made him feel, just a little bit, important. But he could not keep her here, not merely for his own satisfaction. She was weary, and probably hungry, and there was no food to offer her except the various eatables that were sold here. He would not plunder *those* without permission, and anyway, they would make a poor meal. Tiny bite-sized cakes made from clouds and sunlight, as far as Florian could tell from their appearance and texture; pungent sweetmeats wrapped in sugar-veined leaves; bonbons and comfits and pearl-jellies… delicious, in all probability, but not at all sustaining.

'I'll find my way,' said Margot, with that ironic curl to her smile that he never knew how to interpret. He only bowed. She hesitated over the coat, still draped upon one arm. 'I will leave this here, but where shall it be safe?'

Florian found her an empty store-box to pack the coat into, and she laid it inside with tender care and some regret. It was a pretty thing, but Florian had not previously realised that she cared for fripperies; the skirts and bodices she favoured were colourful but always plain and sensible, devoid of the frills and lace and ribbons that decked the clothing of many other women. She wore her leaf-coloured hair bound up, though it did work rather hard to escape, and he did not remember ever seeing any jewellery on her. But perhaps her choices were driven by necessity, for she spent all the hours of her days engaged in some form of labour.

He tucked the idea away.

Margot added Rozebaiel's ribbon and the book, and Florian contributed the mist-trinket, the bottle with the elixir, and the neckcloth. They closed the lid on this collection of oddities, and stacked the box with the others.

Then Margot smiled upon him, the first time she had done so — properly done so — all day. 'Will you be all right here alone?'

Unused to such care, Florian did not know what to say. He hoped it was not a motherly sort of concern she was expressing, and he hoped that the blush he could feel rising in his cheeks did not show too much on his face. 'Of course!' he said stoutly, and busied himself with making certain that the lid of their store-box was properly closed.

Margot was on the point of leaving when the smile fell from her face, and she said in dismay, 'Oh no! I have left my basket at Landricourt. All my herbs! They will be withered away by the morning.' She hovered, probably turning over in her mind the importance of the herbs against the time-consuming labour of another long walk to Landricourt and back. 'Ah, well,' she sighed, clearly deciding against the latter. 'I can gather them all again tomorrow. Goodnight, Florian.'

The door clicked softly to behind her, and Florian was left alone in the quiet darkness of the emporium.

He was by no means so averse to returning to Landricourt as she, not least because he had meant to do so anyway. He did not feel that his search of the place was complete, and besides, he had searched only in daylight. What might he notice, under the altered light of the Gloaming, that he had not seen before? And would he find Rozebaiel again, still wandering from room to room in her rosy skirts? With the Chanteraines already gone home, he had little else to do; the storeroom was in order, and the shop, apparently, closed early.

His mind made up, he left at once, pausing only to extinguish the lamps and lock up at the back. The alley behind the emporium shone silvery-grey in the gloom, and he always fancied that it looked quite different, somehow — as though it were not the same alley at all but a similar one, transposed over the top. Slightly wider, slightly airier, paved in silver rather than stone. And did the wind coil and whisper down it in a different way than it did in the daytime, or during the night? Once, Florian had been certain that he heard words folded somewhere within the billowings of the wind, though he had not been able to discern what they were.

He had the lamp with him, that Margot had borrowed from the jade parlour. He would use it while he explored, and return it to its proper place when he left. And he would fetch Margot's basket of herbs, too, and deliver it to her on his way home.

Florian made his way first to Morel's bakery, and

there he spent two precious copper coins upon a hearty portion of meat and vegetables wrapped in pastry. His evening repast secured — he could drink from one of the clear streams that ran behind Landricourt — he set his back to the town, and ventured westwards.

Landricourt, too, looked different under the Gloaming. No dark, shadowy pile, as it must appear at night, it was a magical display of velvet-dark shadow and silvery light, all set about with stars. Did it always look so? Mist coiled slowly up its gleaming stone walls, eerily pale, and an odd aroma blew upon the wind. There was something of chocolate about that scent, Florian thought, and smoke, and spice, and flowers; a mad mixture of things he could not hope to identify. The afternoon was still warm, Gloaming notwithstanding, but when Florian arrived before the great house, sweating and out of breath, he found it cool and serene — even chilly, for he shivered in his thin shirt and waistcoat.

The front door was open. Did anybody ever close it? His footsteps echoed hollowly upon the silvered-stone floor of the hall, and a mischievous wisp of wind came sailing through the wide-open door and tousled his hair.

He went first into the cellars, his lantern held high, and retrieved Margot's basket. It was not hard to find, for she had left it with all the other trugs, in the same repository for flowers and rosehips which he had himself so often visited that day. He carried it up to the hall and set it by the door, ready to collect upon his departure.

Was it his imagination, or had starlight winked coyly from a distant doorway as he'd returned to the stairs? He retraced his steps and stopped at the bottom of the stairwell, dimming his lantern with his hand.

Not imaginary. There was a glimmer there, almost lost within the depths of the passage's shadows. It beckoned.

Florian followed.

He stepped softly along the echoing passage, ignoring door after door in pursuit of the light. Under the archway of a lost door he went, and into a bare chamber of worn stone that he did not recognise. Had he searched this part of the cellars, earlier in the day? He could not remember.

At first, all was dark. And then came the flicker of light, from the far wall: clear white, and silver-laced, and then mellow blue.

Was it a window there, admitting that light from somewhere outside? No; he did no see a window. He did not see anything, until he crossed the room and raised his lantern high.

A mirror. Its surface rippled like water, and reflected in its depths Florian saw nothing of himself. He saw nothing at all, save a thick white mist, and the light winked again from somewhere deep within.

Was it glass at all? Intrigued, Florian stretched out a hand to touch the curious thing — this, surely, would be of interest to his master! But he had cause to regret his fascination, for his fingers sank into the mirror exactly as though it were water after all, and then the rest of him went, too. He fell helplessly, as though he had thrown himself into the cold embrace of the stream behind the house. Panicking, he struggled, and for a moment he thought he might drown, so hard was it to draw breath.

And then the sensation of falling was over, and he was no longer in the echoing cellar room. He did not know *where* he was, for all around him was broad daylight, and there was no sign of the mirror.

PART THREE

ORIANE

CHAPTER ONE

They did not make wine in this other Landricourt, nor rosewater either.

It seemed a waste to Oriane, for the house was as full of abundant blooms as the Landricourt she knew. And what vivid hues, and such fragrance! She felt sure they would produce a wine of exceptional flavour, and lamented to see them left ungathered.

She had raised the matter, once, with the gentleman in the plum-coloured coat, but he had given it short shrift. 'It is useless,' he had said in his cool way, and refused to be further drawn on the subject.

'What matter that?' Oriane had replied. 'Of what use is wine ever supposed to be?' But this question had gone unanswered.

She was more tolerated than welcomed. Her appearance there had been greeted with no surprise at all, to her puzzlement, but she could interest nobody in the problem of her much-desired return. 'There is no way back,' she was repeatedly told, by men and women alike, their eyes quickly sliding from her face, their minds obviously focused upon anything but the mild inconvenience of her involuntary intrusion. They left her to her own devices, neither seeking to make her comfortable nor attempting to evict her, and so she had blended herself into their strange way of life as best she could, and tried not to repine too much for her home.

The first hours of her strange new life passed in discomfort, unease and the pain of repeatedly dashed hopes. She spent it in a frenzy of activity, searching all over the manor and as far beyond it as she dared go for a way to return to her own little cottage and the pale roses of the Landricourt that she knew. But at last she was forced to accept that they were perfectly right: the mirror in the cellar was gone, and there was no other way home.

Only then, exhausted and distressed, did she contrive to collect herself, and to seek the calm resignation that had often supported her before. Oriane Travere was known as the woman to seek in a crisis. She did not panic, she did not lose her wits or her good sense; indeed, she tended to be particularly blessed with these qualities at times of difficulty.

Well, she needed them now. She thrust away the fear that fluttered in her belly, silenced the voice in her mind that shrieked incoherently of disaster and ruin, and gathered her composure until she could wear it like a cloak, or a mask. And then, at last, she had leisure to look about herself, and consider.

It soon began to strike her that, however involuntary and inconvenient her absence from home might be, and however troubling the apparent impossibility of making any return, she had been granted an uncommon opportunity to explore a highly interesting place. Its differences and its similarities to the manor she knew were equally profound, and equally striking.

There was the matter of the light. Her first

headlong rush through the halls of Landricourt had been accomplished in blinking confusion, for it was as brightly-lit there as it had been dark at home. Why?

Then there was the season, for she had left the sweltering heat of high summer behind. This place, for all its excess of sunlit hours, lay under the deepest chill of winter. At first, her heart pounding and the blood rushing wildly through her body, her eyes meeting new surprises and questions and alarms everywhere she looked, she had hardly noticed the cold. But with her restored calm came an immediate awareness that she was half-frozen, and she began to shiver so hard her teeth chattered. The layers of green linen that made up her summer gown could do nothing to ward off the freezing draughts that drifted down the passages and seeped in through the windows. Rigid with cold, arms wrapped tightly around herself in a futile attempt to conserve warmth, she paused at last to take note of where she had ended up.

A high ceiling arced overhead, elaborately decorated with paintings of lush, pastoral serenity. A rambling thicket of roses climbed up — or down? — the far wall. Three long windows lit the wall, filled with odd, watered glass cut in tiny squared panes. Airy curtains of blue silk framed them, and a vast, intricate rug covered most of a pale stone floor. At one end of the room stood a velvet chaise longue surrounded by matched chairs; at the other stood a large table draped in frothy lace, its surface cluttered with glass decanters and painted cups.

A cross between a drawing-room and some manner of parlour? The chamber seemed undecided as to its function. Oriane had wandered too far and in too much confusion; she could not now determine where she stood in the house.

So frozen was she, the spill of lace over the table looked to her most appealing. She could snatch it up and wrap herself in it, perhaps her shivering would ease—

'Wist!' came a voice from the arched doorway, and a woman stopped upon the threshold. She fixed great dark eyes upon the trembling figure of Oriane and looked her over, her surprise deepening into dismay. 'Sooth, again, is it?' she said upon a sigh, and advanced into the room. 'Still, it has been long since the last time. And you cannot help it, can you, poor dove?' She was as oddly attired as everybody else Oriane had seen: her robust figure was arrayed in a full-skirted ivory silk dress abundant with lace, a fluttering scarf of something indigo and impossibly gauzy trailing from her throat. She wore lilies tucked into her amber-coloured hair, and her eyes were as deep and dark as the sea at night. But traces of a ready smile hung about her full mouth, and despite their unnerving intensity her eyes were kind.

The look of consternation upon the newcomer's face could not lift Oriane's flagging spirits, though the benignity of her words went some way towards mending the impression. And so grateful was she for a little kindness, or any attention at all, that she would have borne a great deal more for it. 'Oh, ma'am!' said she, with a sensation of relief, 'Can you, then, tell me where I am, or how I came to be here? Do I understand that such a thing has happened before?'

The woman went to the table and extracted one of the bottles that stood upon it. It was empty, but she unstoppered it and tipped it up over one of the cups anyway, crowning this inexplicable mime by carefully stoppering the bottle again and carrying the cup to Oriane. 'Drink it all down, dear,' she instructed.

Oriane took the cup doubtfully and peeped into it. 'But there is nothing in it to drink,' said she.

Those deep, dark eyes twinkled with a tolerant mirth. 'You try it and see.'

Oriane tipped up the cup, feeling a fool, but something shifted against her lips after all: a slow, airy current like a breath of summer wind, warm and inviting. She had never thought to drink the wind before, but she found it quite achievable in this place; a fragrant warmth poured down her throat and spread quickly into her frigid limbs, relaxing every muscle with a delicious sun-baked languor. 'Oh,' said Oriane, her lips trembling, and she was loath, then, to hand back the cup.

Her rescuer laughed, and gently took it from her. 'One of Walkelin's better confections, I have always thought. You feel better.' This was a statement, not a question, accompanied by a quick once-over and an approving nod. 'You will need better garments. Poor child, did you not think to ask?'

Oriane hesitated, torn between too many jumbled thoughts. Child? She was nothing of the kind, being over her fortieth year! This lady did not appear to be much older. Who was Walkelin, and what was it that she had just drunk? And who was she supposed to have asked for clothes? Confused, she fell back upon her original question. 'Ma'am. Where is it that I am come to?'

'Why, you are in Laendricourt, of course! And you came, I suppose, by mirror! It has puzzled the Fashioners this age and more, for none of them will own to having wrought it, you see. Some would like the thing *un*wrought again, but others call for more to be made, and it being such a disobedient thing! Comes and goes at will and does just as it likes, and never thinks to ask the likes of you or me if we'd like to be tossed about house to house like leaves on the wind. And you won't find much of a welcome, poor dove, for it's Rozebaiel that's gone the other way, and that's set the cat among the birds.'

Oriane heard this speech with growing befuddlement, which must have shown upon her face, for the lady smiled more kindly upon her, and ceased the flow of words. 'Poor child, I can see I am only confusing you. I am Nynevarre, and you may rely on me to see to it that you don't starve to death. How are you called?'

'Oriane Travere,' she replied, though without much hope of being attended to. When she had given her name before, at the invitation of the velvet-coated man, he had returned only a look of indifference and dismissed her from his notice.

Nynevarre was as good as her word, however, and advanced upon Oriane with a promising bustle. She was not looking at Oriane, though; her eyes scanned the roses that clambered up the walls, and as she passed a tangle of particularly plump blossoms her hand darted out and plucked one, two, three of them. 'You may always ask the roses, dear, if you are in need, for they do like to help. Though whether they will do so with Rozebaiel gone, who can say? Shall we try? Velvet, sweet thing, and warm! Any colour you like, to fit this lady.' Upon these words she threw the first of the roses gently into the air, and down came a gown. It was velvet indeed, coloured the same plums-in-wine hue of the cold gentleman's coat, and by far the finest thing Oriane had ever seen. 'Oh, how exact!' congratulated Nynevarre, and threw up a second rose, and then the third. 'Boots, silk-lined and ribbon-tied! And the very warmest shawl you can contrive, dears.' Both of these articles descended in their turn. The pair of dark leather boots landed upon the stone floor with a clatter, trailing silver ribbons all about, and a thick shawl of something that looked like moss drifted slowly down, its luscious folds tinted the colour of dark grapes. When Oriane, with trembling fingers, picked up the latter, she found to her amazement that it felt as much like moss as it looked, excepting the lining of silky-soft something that covered its underside.

Oriane stared at Nynevarre, unable to speak.

'Well? Dress quickly, dear. Walkelin's brew will last you a good while yet, but you don't want to be underclad when it wears off.'

Oriane collected herself, and remembered to express her thanks. This Nynevarre waved away, and she busied herself about the table-top while Oriane exchanged her old cotton dress for the exquisite velvet one, slid the boots onto her feet, and wrapped the delicate shawl around her shoulders. She stood a moment in awkwardness, feeling five times too fine and not at all herself. But the delicious fabrics imparted such warmth and — did she imagine it? — such serenity, that she soon lost her reserve.

'You feel better,' said Nynevarre again, looking Oriane over with approval. She abandoned the table, which she had set into much better order than it had been in when Oriane had come in, and held out her hands in a kindly fashion. 'Come, dove, I will find you a nook. You are tired, and may wish soon to sleep?'

'Please,' Oriane replied, abruptly aware of a crushing weariness. Perhaps it was the warmth still coiling through her body from Walkelin's peculiar drink, or the sheer relief of being offered assistance, but a great yawn overtook her and all at once she could hardly keep her eyes open. She followed Nynevarre obediently, passing out of the parlour-drawing-room and into a corridor painted up like a grove of winding trees, their boughs hanging low with a heavy burden of fruit. Some of those fruits looked real enough that she could almost fancy she could reach out and take one—

'Here,' said Nynevarre and did just that, plucking an apple from the wall and handing it off to Oriane. She repeated this manoeuvre at intervals as they traversed two winding corridors, passed through an elegant saloon hung with bejewelled silks and a peculiar room directly adjacent which seemed given over entirely to the storage of a thousand, many-coloured coats, and finally went up three flights of stairs. At the top of the third flight Oriane was mildly surprised to see an expanse of plain wall, painted white, and apparently offering no unusual function. But Nynevarre applied her fingers to the bland surface and curled them up, tugging and teasing at the paint until a length of white fabric came free. A nightgown. She laid this over the top of the armful of fruit and flowers Oriane was already holding, and opened the plain wooden door that stood at the top of the stairs. Beyond it Oriane glimpsed a bedchamber of blessed simplicity compared with the bizarre array below: it held a narrow bed with an embroidered white counterpane, an oaken chest set at the foot, and a rug of red rags covering the wood-panelled floor.

'I'll come for you in the morning,' said Nynevarre with an inviting tilt of her head towards the open doorway. 'You'll sleep well.'

This last was stated with confidence. To Oriane's relief, once she had quietly thanked her hostess, gone alone into the room and changed into her new nightgown, she lay down upon the soft little bed and promptly proved Nynevarre's assurance fully justified.

CHAPTER TWO

The morning came, but Nynevarre did not.

Oriane woke to a heavy grey sky, rain-infused and swollen with clouds. The biting chill of her room took her by surprise as she threw back the counterpane, accustomed as her body was to the soporific heat of summer. She did not instantly recall the events of the day before, but when her gaze fell upon the velvet gown and the mossy shawl that lay carefully spread upon the chest at the foot of her bed, memory awoke.

She dressed quickly, shivering, and neatened her hair as best she could without the aid of either a mirror or a hair brush. Her mind, she found, did not want to dwell too closely upon her predicament, or the extreme strangeness of her surroundings. Since her tranquillity was best preserved by following its dictates she kept her thoughts focused upon the simple things: buttoning up her gown and lacing her boots, smoothing the caramel-coloured coils of her hair, tucking the thick, dark shawl around her chilled arms. Thus attired, she waited some time longer, trusting in the imminent arrival of Nynevarre, for the brightness of the sky told her that the morning was some way advanced. She spent the time in consuming the remainder of the fruit she had been given the night before, thus silencing the uncomfortable rumblings of her stomach.

At length, when many minutes passed in near silence, no quick step upon the boards outside announcing the approach of a visitor, Oriane abandoned her vigil and ventured out.

The house looked a little different under the more muted light of an ordinary morning. The unnatural brightness of the previous evening was gone, and while the effect was more restful, it also held a degree of oppressive gloom which Oriane's spirits could ill bear. With no fixed idea as to where she might be going or what she hoped to achieve with her wanderings, she simply followed her feet, choosing at random from among the winding passages, twisting turns and inviting doorways that she passed. She felt that she was progressing higher up into the manor, though she did not for some time climb any stairs; the floors sloped, or seemed to do so, and her straining calf-muscles informed her that she was borne steadily upwards. Each window that she passed afforded loftier and loftier views over the grounds that lay beyond the walls, though to her confusion there was little consistency to be discerned among them. Through one, she saw a large wood of trees all hung about with autumnal array, their leaves tinted copper and russet and amber. From another, she saw a long, narrow lake of green water thick with lily pads, and flanked on either side by sparsely-spaced birch trees. The next showed a village of narrow, crowded houses, thatch-roofed and white-painted, each leaning in an entirely different direction to its neighbour. By the time she at last found herself faced with a real staircase leading upwards, she had seen all this and more: an expanse of tumbling hills scattered with every-colour blossoms; a network of little streams like a maze, each running with silvery water and jumping with glittering fish; and, at the last, nothing but an ocean of thick clouds in every shade of silver and grey and white. Bright lightning bolts shot through from time to time, though no echoing rumble of thunder attended the flashes of light.

The stairs coiled into a tight spiral, and raced steeply upwards. Roses clung to the banisters, and the steps themselves had all but disappeared under a carpet of rose-leaves. Oriane climbed slowly up, taking care where she placed her feet upon the slippery leaf-rug. But her boots served her well, her feet did not slip, and she achieved the top of the staircase without incident.

A howling wind was blowing down the corridor at the top, not a wisp of which she had felt from the bottom of the stairs. The current blew back her hair, tried to race away with her shawl; she clutched the latter more tightly about her. The corridor was flooded with pale morning light, but she could not see where it came from; there was too much light, or too much wind, or some other obstruction. She paused a moment in thought; then, deciding that the source of the wind was likely to prove the more interesting object, she set her face to the gale and strode determinedly forward.

A scant moment later, a door materialised upon her left. It stood open. The room beyond was not the source of the wind, for that swirled ever onward, emanating from some other destination somewhere ahead. But intriguing sounds reached her ears from within: an odd clatter as of machinery, someone muttering under his breath in words she could not understand, and the *drip-drip-drop* as of water trickling from a great height.

'Hello?' Oriane called, unwilling to intrude herself without invitation. But whether the wind carried her words away from the ears of the muttering gentleman, or whether he were too absorbed in his activities to pay her any heed, she could not tell. She only knew that no answer was returned.

She knocked upon the open door and went cautiously in, taking care that the soles of her boots should make a noise upon the bare stone floor. None of these efforts availed her much. The tower-room's occupant stood with his back to her, intent upon a flurry of rapid-moving machinery before him, and he neither turned nor looked round as Oriane went in.

The room reminded her of the turrets at the Landricourt she knew, at least in shape and proportion. Unusually spacious, its rounded stone walls were clad in rose-vines like the towers of her memory, though these came in many another colour: the blue of cornflowers, violet-purple, amber and marigold, and still more. The gale had not entered here, but many of its gentler siblings had: stray breezes coiled about the floor, wisps tugged at her hair, and the air sang with the melodies of rampant winds. The three long windows each held a different view: the left showed the green-tinted lake she had seen on the way up, the right a vision of a ruined ballroom hung with ragged tapestries, and the centre

— the largest by far — looked out upon that sea of lightning-split clouds.

'Forgive me,' said Oriane, raising her voice to make herself heard above the mechanical clatter of rolling gears. 'I do not mean to intrude, only, I am a newcomer here and in trying to find my way about I appear to have stumbled upon your work-room. I do not suppose you might be able to assist me?'

She might just as well have saved her breath, for she received no more reply than she had before. Intrigued, uncertain, dismayed, she took a step nearer the machine, and bent her gaze upon it. It resembled some manner of loom, she thought, though it was far more complex than any she had seen before. It did not appear to be loaded with anything; no yarn spun upon its shuttles. Nonetheless, a length of fabric was emerging, folds of it draping gauzily to the floor. The stuff was as pale as the clouds she saw arrayed beyond that central window, though laced through with threads as vivid-blue or violet as the roses that clustered across the ceiling. It sparkled with something — something like motes of lightning, she thought with sudden inspiration, though chiding herself for so fanciful a notion directly afterwards.

But then, perhaps it was not so fanciful.

'Forgive me,' Oriane said again, taking a step nearer. 'But are you really weaving the clouds and the lightning into cloth? You are, aren't you?'

'And the wind-song of the roses,' said the man, surprising her. 'Just the two colours, today, though I think of bringing in a third — a waft of summer to warm it up, you understand. It is perhaps a little chilly?' He cast a critical eye over his handiwork, and it *was* wintry, Oriane could not deny. But it was gloriously so, the grey of glistening rain and snow-clouds.

'I couldn't think it necessary,' Oriane said. 'The lightning-sparks save it from insipidity.'

This comment got the weaver's attention as nothing else had done. He looked at her at last, turned to face her, fixing her with a gaze both bright and curious. He was an elderly man by appearance, with skin like a length of rumpled cotton, his hair a shock of white. One eye was clear blue, the other opaque like milk and pearls. His garb showed off the excellence of his craftsmanship, for he wore a shirt of some airy silk that looked spun from summer clouds, and a waistcoat of something mossy and dark, like her own shawl. Only his neckcloth seemed incongruous, for it was a length of plain, drab cotton, somewhat threadbare, its once-white hue darkened to dull ivory with time and use.

'Who are you?' said the man, his loom forgotten.

Oriane explained herself as best she could. Her abrupt appearance and her inability to account for it did not surprise him at all; he was as resigned as Nynevarre, though thankfully he did not seem disposed to dismiss her presence as irrelevant as so many of his fellows had done. 'Aye, you will be confused,' he said when she had finished her speech. 'But Laendricourt has welcomed the likes of you before, and will do so again, I make no doubt.'

'Laendricourt?' echoed she, further puzzled, for the word was so close to the one she knew, and yet not the same. Was it only the odd, lilting accent that coloured his voice, or was the house's name as altered as the building itself? It came to her that she had heard it spoken the same way before. By Nynevarre?

89

'Aye,' he said. 'The Wind's Own Tower, and I am Walkelin.' He surveyed her with a glance that seemed considering. 'Have you any experience at weaving?'

'None, sir. I am a winemaker.'

'Wine?' He spoke the word sharply, and sat straighter in his chair. 'They make the wyne at Landricourt, do they? That is most interesting, madam. Most interesting. I'll ask you all about it, soon enough.'

'I will gladly tell you all I know, sir.'

'That you will, that you will indeed.' His mismatched eyes twinkled at her, and the syllables of his name sounded again in her mind. *Walkelin*. A memory echoed.

'You spin draughts as well, sir, do you not? I had the privilege of sampling one of them last evening, by Nynevarre's direction. Are they cloud-wrought, too?'

'Which one was it?' said he, with a shrewd narrowing of his eyes.

'I do not know its name, sir. A warming elixir, like drinking a waft of hot summer wind.'

'And there you have it! Exactly like, for 'tis what it's made out of. A favourite, that, at this season. Aye, I make 'em — me and Ghislain, that is. I'm a Fashioner, madam, as you must surely have guessed, and 'tis the wind and clouds that I use meself. I'm a rare one, at that. The winds in particular are tricksy things; got to keep an eye on 'em, a close eye, or they'll spoil a fine piece of work in a blink.'

'Is that what became of your neckcloth?'

Walkelin looked down at the item in question, as though he had never seen it before. 'Hm,' said he and unwound it from his neck. He stared at it, ran it through his fingers, and finally laid it, very carefully, upon a nearby table-top. 'No, madam, that is not what became of my neckcloth,' he said thoughtfully, and added, 'Most interesting.' He looked again at her, brighter and more alert than ever, and looked her over. 'Interesting times, methinks,' he observed. 'The Brightening, you know, is gone all awry. Few know it yet, but I do. It's working with air and light up here all day by meself that does it. Sensitive to these things, I am, more so than most, and I tell you: it's awry. They'll all notice, soon. Maybe today, maybe tomorrow.'

'Notice what, sir?' said Oriane. 'What do you mean by the Brightening?'

He gave her a bird-like glance of interest, head tilted. 'Is there no Brightening, where you come from?'

'N-no, nothing like that. Well, that is — there is the Gloaming, which I fancy must be something similar. Only the other way about.'

'Ahh,' said Walkelin, not at all in surprise; rather in recognition. 'Yes, the other way about,' he said cheerfully, and turned back to his loom. 'Exactly the other way! Wait until four, lady-lass, and you'll see.'

He seemed to fall at once into such absorption with his work that he forgot Oriane's presence on the spot. She hesitated, uncertain. His labours excited a powerful curiosity in her, and she wanted to offer herself as assistant — beg him to teach her — anything, provided she received some further glimpse into his mystifying arts. But he was frowning in concentration, busy about the loom, involved in some endeavour that struck her as delicate and complicated, and she could not bring herself to be so rude as to interrupt him again. So she murmured a polite farewell, offered a curtsey which he did not see, and quietly withdrew, promising herself that she would return to the tower soon. Once the Brightening came in, perhaps; she might very reasonably seek his further counsel upon that topic.

CHAPTER THREE

The gale outside the tower-top room had not abated at all, though it had altered. What had been a freezing wind had grown balmy in temperature, and smelled of sun upon the sea. Oriane followed its current back the way she had come, only to find, to her immense surprise, that the staircase was not where she had left it. Where there had been a way down, there was now a blank stone wall.

'I suppose,' said she, after a moment's silent astonishment, 'that if one may catch the winds in this peculiar place and weave the breezes into shawls, then a staircase may grow tired of always being in one spot, and take itself exploring instead.' All of which might be quite reasonable according to the rules of Laendricourt, but the reflection did not in any way resolve the problem of how to get down, for a quick search of the environs soon confirmed her worst fears: there were no other stairs.

She was still stationed before that disobliging wall, paralysed with indecision, when Walkelin's voice came drifting down the passage behind her, carried by the sea winds. 'Have the stairs jaunted off? Only wait a moment, good lady, and they will return.'

Oriane, turning to look, caught a glimpse of his tufted white head vanishing back through the door to his workroom — he had put his face around the door-frame just to speak to her, and immediately gone back again.

And when she turned about, there they were, meekly materialising out of nowhere. There came a grinding of stone upon stone as the wall slunk away — to where, she wondered? Had it, too, abandoned its more regular position in order to take up a station here? Were the various parts of Laendricourt all in the daily habit of taking refreshing holidays in other parts of the house? But there were the stairs, and down them she went — quickly, in case they should prove fickle, and dart off again to somewhere else.

Either they had, or there was some far stranger explanation at work, for upon reaching the foot of the stairs Oriane found herself somewhere unexpected. It was not the simple stone hall she had passed through on the way up, but rather a deliciously warm kitchen, smelling of bread and beer and fruit. She had not felt the stairs move, and began to wonder whether they did so at all. Perhaps it was simply that the top steps sometimes led into different places, and the bottom ones also. Just now the bottom step clearly fancied the kitchen, and she could hardly blame it.

The room was almost deserted, which seemed strange; the heavy mix of aromas upon the air suggested a large staff hard at work. The ovens pumped out a fierce heat, and an enormous fire occupied most of one wall, roaring splendidly even without any obvious attendance. The only person in charge of all this industry and splendour was asleep, however: a large lady, she sat perched atop a tall stool before a great work-table, her cheek pressed to the age-roughened oak boards and her eyes firmly shut. Oriane heard a snore.

She did not trouble to wake the lady but went to the door, suppressing the temptation to go in search of the fresh bread she could smell. Nynevarre's fruits, however marvellous, could not long sustain her.

Beyond the kitchen was a parlour quite filled with people. It was a fine parlour, hung with silvery drapes, its ceiling carved and painted in glittering splendour. Far too fine a room to be adjacent to all the strong smells and (usually) noisy clatter of a kitchen, she thought; but when she turned her head to glance once again into that room, there was no kitchen at all, only an empty stone hall again.

'Ah! And there you are,' came Nynevarre's voice, and there was Nynevarre herself, bustling up to welcome Oriane. 'I did come to fetch you, my dear, only I was a trifle late, and then I could not trace you. Whisked away, were you not? Perhaps lost? It can be difficult to find your way about when first you arrive, poor dear, for the changes take some getting used to.'

'I found my way up to Walkelin's tower,' said Oriane, surreptitiously surveying the other occupants of the parlour. 'He was kind to me, though very busy, I think. And after that the stairs would not immediately agree to bring me down again.' She received a few curious glances from some few of the people arrayed about in deep, comfortable chairs, or seated around a lace-clad table playing cards, though nobody spoke to her. She noticed, slightly to her discomfort, the man in the plum velvet coat. He did not choose to maintain his earlier indifference, however, for his eyes were fixed upon her with a degree of intense fascination she found both unnerving and intriguing. So eagerly did he now scrutinise her that she wondered whether his previous dismissal of her had been at all sincere, or some kind of act; for when he realised that his notice of her was observed by the other card-players at the table, he quickly withdrew his gaze, and did not look at her again.

Curious.

'I will show you about, shall I?' said Nynevarre, and tucked her arm through Oriane's. 'After all, since you will be with us for some time, we cannot have you wandering lost and starving to death. Only we will not go too far from the house — no one does, you know, for it is dangerous beyond the walls. We will begin with the dining parlour, that will be best.' So saying, she swept Oriane towards the door — different from the one Oriane had come through, on the other side of the room — and kept up a congenial flow of good-natured conversation all the while. But they had not got more than halfway across the pretty green-carpeted saloon beyond before the quick steps of someone in a hurry were heard behind them, and a deep voice spoke.

'My good madam, if I may detain you? I shall not keep her long, Nynevarre.'

Madam? She had not heard that form of address since she had come through the mirror, and the word alone was sufficient to stop her. Politely she disentangled her arm from Nynevarre's and turned back, to find the man in the plum velvet coat standing there. He carried some knitted woollen garment over one arm.

'Quickly, Ghislain!' said Nynevarre. 'Cannot you see that she is famished?'

Ghislain bowed, and held out his burden to Oriane. It was a shawl, and a familiar one. Taking it with fingers that very slightly shook, she was soon confirmed in her suspicion: it was her own shawl, her favourite, knitted by her own hands in her preferred shade of blue. 'But,' said she in great confusion, 'I was not wearing it when I — I had left this at home, I am quite sure that I — how did it come to be here?' She fixed Ghislain with a swift, penetrating look and said, more coherently, 'How, sir, did you come to realise that it was mine?'

'I imagined it must be, Madame Travere. Who else could it possibly belong to?' With which words he gave a cursory bow, and left again. Oriane could only stare after him, wondering.

'How nice it is to have one's own things about one!' said Nynevarre brightly, and took up Oriane's arm again. 'It is fortunate that the thing should have come through after you, though I should like to know who has lost a shawl or a coat or some other such thing today! They will be less happy, I am sure, but no matter. It cannot be held to be any fault of yours. The dining parlour, my dear. Just this way. Through the saloon and over the threshold of the third door, the one behind the quartz pillar there. That's it. If you should chance to step through and find the scullery instead, or a garret, just go back over once or twice more and you shall be safely delivered. Yes, here we are. The table, dear, always set and ready. Just lift the lids of the dishes, and take whatever you like. The kitchens deliver promptly. There! Trout in cream! And onions in sugar, and new bread. Very fine.'

The dining room was as splendid as the card parlour, though in a more muted way. Clad in red-toned wood and lit by four vast windows, it was dominated by a table still more enormous even than the one Oriane had passed in the kitchen. This table was spread with an ivory brocade cloth and cluttered up with serving-mats, and every inch of its surface was crowded over with silver serving dishes. Nynevarre had merely investigated the contents of the nearest three, but Oriane amused herself for some little time in exploring further. She found every delicacy that might be supposed to please: stewed chicken in wine, buttered crab, a ham pie, a trifle of quinces and apples and custard, white soup and pease pottage, griddle cakes and buns, pickled mushrooms and a breathtakingly delicate tart filled with fruit jelly and almonds. Each seemed freshly baked, the hot dishes still steaming. She soon learned to restrain her explorations, however, for when she returned to the dish that had held the ham pie she found it now to contain a dish of scallops instead, and the tart had vanished in favour of a currant cheesecake.

'Changefulness is the way of Laendricourt,' said Nynevarre peaceably, seating herself at the table with a plate of trout-in-cream. 'When you find something you like, dear, it's wise to partake of it at once.'

'And why is it?' said Oriane, cheerfully contenting herself with the scallops and the cheesecake. 'Changeful, I mean.'

Nynevarre did not precisely know, as indicated by a shrug of her shoulders as she applied herself to her food. 'Some say as there's been too much magic done here for far too long. It's seeped into the very walls, and will not come out again.' She chewed a portion of fish, and further remarked, 'Myself, I would certainly say as there's too much magic about, one way or another. There's Rozebaiel, after all, and Mistral, and even Walkelin in his way.'

Oriane thought, all at once, of Pharamond, and wondered what he would make of this odd but marvellous place. His emporium would fit in seamlessly. She wondered with a pang what he thought of her disappearance, and quickly turned her thoughts away again. Rozebaiel. She had heard that name mentioned before. 'Who is she?' Oriane said. 'Rozebaiel, that is.'

'Oh,' said Nynevarre with a considering look. 'No, you wouldn't have met her, at that. They say she wasn't born, exactly, though I can't see as how anybody knows for sure. But that she was found as an infant all swaddled in rose-leaves is beyond doubt. And Mistral sailed into the south-east tower one day, borne by a fine breeze, or so they say. He's lived there ever since, and the winds, too.'

'The Wind's Own Tower,' said Oriane.

Nynevarre nodded. ''Tis his magic that gives Walkelin the means to weave as he does, though there's much credit to be given to his own art, too. Now, with Rozebaiel gone, some say as the roses will wither up and die, and then where will we be? And if Mistral goes, too!' Nynevarre illustrated this point with a sad shake of her head, and finished with a large bite of trout.

Oriane mused over this in silence, and arrived at one or two conclusions. 'Is that why I am not given much welcome?'

'Paltry, to think it your fault that Rozebaiel should be gone! Only it is not quite a random thing, and that's known. There was a mirror, was there not?'

Oriane nodded.

'And you approached?'

'I did. I could not help it. I felt… drawn.'

Nynevarre nodded wisely. 'No one ever appears without that someone else goes the other way. Tis the way of it. And to the minds of *some,* since it's you that must have fallen into the mirror, it is your doing that Rozebaiel is taken from us.' She spoke sympathetically, but there was a hard glint to her eye that caused Oriane to wonder whether Nynevarre did not, in fact, rather agree with these other people.

Was it really true, that Rozebaiel and Mistral were of such paramount importance? Would Walkelin's soothing draughts be impossible to make, without Mistral's winds? Would the roses continue so obliging, under the prolonged absence of Rozebaiel? Perhaps, but perhaps not. *Magic has seeped into the walls,* Nynevarre had said, and Oriane felt that she was right.

Only not, perhaps, always — or not without softening influence. Oriane's quick mind grasped another subtlety: that when she had arrived the night before, the house of Laendricourt had been by no means so chaotic. She had wandered its passages and halls largely in peace, without the disruptions of staircases wandering about and doors opening onto the wrong rooms — or tapestries growing bored of their general configurations and resolving themselves into new scenes entirely, as she now saw happening upon the wall of the dining-parlour. The difference was the light: yester eve there had been the

Brightening, and now there was not.

Oriane's musings released her long enough for her to remember her food, and she took a bite of scallops. They tasted of jugged hare.

Noting her look of surprise, Nynevarre eyed the offending dish and suggested: 'If it's scallops you were after, you might try the beef.'

Tentatively, Oriane tested the currant cheesecake. It savoured strongly of apples, and had the texture of a baked pudding.

'I do not know where the cheesecake might be got to,' said Nynevarre vaguely. 'I found it in a trifle, once, and another time as a honey tart.'

'Is that trout you are eating?' said Oriane.

'I believe it is pigeon.' Nynevarre took another bite, chewed slowly, and then said: 'Or partridge. It is difficult to be sure.'

Nynevarre's tour was not, in the end, of much use, for by its close Oriane felt more confused than ever. All the doors led to three or four different destinations at least, and it was a mere matter of chance as to which one would be found upon the other side. The stairs were all in the habit of twisting themselves about until top and bottom came out someplace else; one elegant marble staircase had its roots in the great hall in Laendricourt's west wing, but when Oriane and Nynevarre arrived at the top they found themselves deposited in a small library, which Nynevarre said was quite on the other side of the house. Upon the return journey, they came out in a charming pillared folly situated just off the kitchen garden, and had to forge through freezing winds and a haze of snow to re-enter the house. Oriane quickly concluded that she would just have to accustom herself to being lost.

'The Light will soon come in,' said Nynevarre, rather confusing Oriane. A glance at the silver watch that hung from her belt and a nod of satisfaction followed. 'Half past one. I've work about the house, but I will call for you at four?'

She bustled off without much waiting for a reply, leaving Oriane alone in a cool pantry well-stocked with jars.

Oriane did not mind the solitude. Nynevarre was kind, but there was a bustle and a hurry about her which did not suit Oriane's more measured pace for long, and she talked on at such a speed that Oriane began to feel quite tired by it. She took a moment to breathe and calm her mind, relishing the restful quiet of the pantry, before she ventured to step across the threshold into whatever lay beyond.

It proved to be a storage room, dimly lit, its walls stacked high with boxes of every shape, size and hue. In the centre stood a long-legged table, books piled upon its surface. It could almost be the twin of Pharamond's; the thought flitted across her mind and was dismissed before it could cause her any pain. Nonetheless, her heart twisted in her breast and she had a moment's work to dismiss likewise the visage of Pharamond himself, his eyes warm with approval in the way he often looked at her...

She heard voices from an adjacent room, and instantly composed herself to be quiet. The interruption was of use to her; all thoughts fled her mind at once, leaving her focused upon the task of removing herself without disturbing those who, presumably, owned the space. She was on the point of leaving again when a little ruckus reached her ears: a thumping and clattering noise, quite impossible to identify. She looked around.

One of the boxes was rocking about. It jumped and jumped, striving, apparently, to throw itself off the stack of store-boxes upon which it rested — a mission it shortly achieved, landing with a smack upon the floor. Whereupon it immediately began to twitch and shuffle and writhe its way towards Oriane, lid rattling.

Oriane did not know how to respond to such an overture, for she had never before been importuned by a store-box. She stood, undecided, and expecting any moment that whoever stood in the adjacent room must hear the noise and come in. This thought almost sent her fleeing out of the room at once, for how could she explain her presence in what appeared to be a private store? But no footsteps approached; there was a hubbub of voices, raised in some manner of disagreement, and they were too absorbed by their conversation to notice much besides.

The box reached her feet and began to hurl itself against her shoe, over and over. Oriane could not ignore such an entreaty. She bent and removed the lid, which action the box greeted with a kind of sigh of relief.

A peculiar array of objects lay inside. There was a mass of gauzy mauve fabric stitched in silver, so airy that it might have been woven from the clouds. It must be Walkelin's work, thought Oriane. A length of ribbon lay on top, glittering with fresh rain, and with it a puff of glassy cloud — or was it misty glass?

And a neckcloth, amber-bright and made, ostensibly, from rose petals.

The neckcloth leapt into her hands and would not consent to be put down again. Nor did she wish to, for her thoughts flew to the incongruously plain article around Walkelin's neck, and his obvious astonishment at finding it there. She remembered also the puzzling appearance of her own shawl at Laendricourt, and Nynevarre's remark. *I should like to know who has lost a shawl or a coat or some other such thing.* The neckcloth was Walkelin's, doubtless; but how came it to be here in Laendricourt after all?

She must return it to Walkelin, whatever the circumstances of its residence here, and it certainly seemed most desirable that she should do so. Oriane waited, in case any of the other objects in the box should wish to be taken away likewise. They lay quiescent, however — slightly to her regret, for the ribbon was the most beautiful she had ever set eyes upon — and she replaced the lid upon the box. A moment's work saw it placed back upon the stack where it lived, and out she went, carrying the neckcloth with her.

The door led her into a serene morning-room with windows of green stained glass, and a pale, feathery carpet. A large sofa beckoned, clad sumptuously in dark green, and she sank gratefully into it, requiring a moment's rest to compose herself. Had she really just entered somebody's store-room and robbed it of a neckcloth? She could not be certain that it belonged to Walkelin. Even if it did, what had it been doing in that box? Who had put it there? Had she done more harm than good in removing it? Perhaps she had just disgracefully thieved the thing.

But she had not tried to. It had foisted itself upon her, and she doubted not that she was chosen as messenger, not thief. All she could do was ensure the neckcloth was taken to Walkelin — provided she could find her way back to the Wind's Tower. The Brightening would soon come, and if she was not mistaken in her surmise, it would bring with it a more rational arrangement of the house. But what use was that? She had found the tower by mistake, and during the natural light of the day. What road could she take to find it again, if she were to try?

There followed a half-hour of pure confusion, for door after door carried Oriane through such a dizzying succession of disparate chambers that she was left at a loss. Nor could she retrace her steps, for returning back the way she had come never did take her *back* anywhere; there was only onward and ever onward, and never where she wanted to go. Exasperated and increasingly chilled, she draped the neckcloth around her own neck to keep it safe and tucked her frozen hands under the folds of her shawls. She was wearing two: her own woollen shawl over her gown, and the moss-made one over the top of that. The extra warmth thawed her stiffened fingers, and she was able to face the next chamber and the next with a somewhat renewed equanimity.

So many different places had she visited in such quick succession that she had all but stopped paying attention to what any of them were like; she paused long enough only to note that this, still, was *not* the Wind's Tower, and on she went. But at length she was obliged to stop, for upon entering an odd, echoing room with a domed roof, no windows and too many sides, dominated by a very strange clock, she found that the door through which she had entered was not at all disposed to let her leave again.

Upon turning and attempting to step back over the threshold, she found herself walking nose-first into a mirror. Its blank, hard surface glittered in cold mockery of her confusion. *Blank.* It did not reflect her own figure, though she stood directly before it.

Shocked, she turned again, eyes scanning the room for signs of some other egress. There were none. There was nothing there at all, in fact; the floor was a bare expanse of polished, patterned bronze, the pale walls fitted with curving pillars of the same, and the ceiling adorned only with three globes of light. All that there was of any interest was the clock, and when another attempt at departure ended with the same, dispiriting result, Oriane felt obliged to focus upon the clock instead.

It was a handsome specimen, to say the least. The tallest clock she had ever beheld, it towered almost as high as the high-domed ceiling, its faces looking down upon Oriane with a kind of chilly indifference. Really, the clock seemed almost aware, and not in an especially good mood.

And how many faces it had! Walking slowly around it, Oriane counted thirty-seven of them, all displaying different times. The clock was built out of reddish-coloured wood, or something like it, its pale faces glittering with light and magic and jewels. Some of the second-hands were racing around at a speed Oriane was unused to seeing in a clock; others crept in agonisingly slow circles, barely making any progress at all.

Half of them had stopped completely. This did not seem right to Oriane's practical frame of mind. Had nobody been tending to the glorious thing? What a great shame that was. It took her a moment to identify any apparent means of winding it up, but at last she found it: a great bronze key, half hidden in between three closely-crowded clock faces. This she grasped and turned, relieved to find that it turned easily enough under her hands.

Almost immediately, the air resounded with the sounds of tick-ticking hands spurred into renewed activity. The groaning of gears accompanied the noise, and such a clatter went up that Oriane wanted to clap her hands over her ears to keep it out. But she kept grimly at her work, and wound the clock until it would go no further. Then she stepped back, pleased with the results of her labours, and stood a while watching the hands upon the various clock-faces spinning merrily about. They were still not at all regular, to her disappointment; they all ran at different speeds, marking different times. But perhaps that was how it was meant to be.

A few minutes later, the clock began to chime. The noise reverberated around the room at such volume that Oriane could barely stand it; she *did* cover her ears this time, and fell afterwards to the floor, curling herself up and throwing her shawls over her head in an effort to mute the terrible racket.

Happily, she was not long tormented. The clock chimed once; twice; three times! And then fell silent.

She was reminded of the way a clock's chime sounded across Argantel, when the Gloaming came in. But there were four chimes then, always, so it could not be the same.

Could it? For the quality of the light was changing in the room, growing — almost imperceptibly — lighter and brighter, but with a brittle quality to it that she recognised. Was the Brightening come in? She could feel no doubt that it *was,* and tried to persuade herself that there had been four chimes, not three, and she had somehow miscounted.

A glance at her own pocket-watch dispelled any such comforting ideas: it was but three o'clock. Nynevarre had said four, hadn't she? The light was an hour early.

Oriane began to tremble, her watch almost dropping from her shaking hands. Hastily she packed it away, and tried hard to calm herself. She could not have altered the ages-long flow of time across Argantel, could she? Not merely by winding a clock?

But she had. Surely, there could be no other explanation; it could not be a coincidence. What had she done? And what would it mean for Laendricourt?

PART FOUR
FLORIAN

CHAPTER ONE

Beyond the mirror was no cellar room, like the one Florian had just left. He fetched up instead somewhere very high up, though he could not immediately have said how he knew anything about his relative elevation, for he there were no windows looking out over a landscape some way below. He was in somebody's wardrobe, the kind that consists of a smallish room lined wall-to-wall with cupboards. Some of the doors hung open, affording Florian a view of many racks of garments, all sumptuously coloured and finely made.

He could not find the door.

There were mirrors, though, mirrors aplenty. At least three at first count, not including any that might be concealed behind the carved, dark wooden cupboard-doors that all hung open. Was that a lazy habit, or was somebody in the process of choosing—

'Another one,' said a deep voice, and Florian, with a sinking heart, discovered himself to be correct upon the latter point. Spinning about in search of the source of those low, pleasant tones, he saw a tall gentleman with the silvery-white hair of advanced age, though his face did not look so very old, nor was his posture that of an elderly man. Prematurely white, perhaps; it happened to some. He was in the region of fifty, maybe fifty-five. His cool grey eyes, were fixed upon Florian with a questioning look, and his mouth was rather grim. He was a well-groomed specimen, and appeared to be changing his dress, for a reddish-purple velvet coat was in the process of being returned to a nearby cupboard, and his dark silken waistcoat was unbuttoned.

'Another one?' Florian echoed. 'Is this, then, what became of Oriane?'

The gentleman did not immediately answer, being engaged in laying his coat very tenderly upon a hanger carved of wood, and depositing it into the dark, welcoming recess before him. This done, he removed his waistcoat and gave it the same treatment, then turned a stern eye upon Florian. 'Madame Travere is here, yes,' he finally replied. 'I can answer for it that she was well, perhaps an hour or two ago.'

Florian felt a flicker of excitement, and congratulated himself for his good fortune. To tumble, quite by chance, through the very same portal which had stolen Margot's friend! Perhaps he would be the means of shepherding her home again, and would find himself in high favour as a consequence. These pleasing thoughts warmed his heart, and he answered in high good cheer: 'Excellent! If you would be so kind to direct me to her, Seigneur, then neither of us shall much longer impose upon you.'

The gentleman looked at him strangely. 'You have a way, then, of returning yourselves to Argantel?'

'Why,' said Florian, experiencing for the first time a whisper of doubt, 'One of these mirrors was the means of getting me here, wasn't it? I should think it would work in reverse?'

A glint of cool grey amusement was his answer, and his confidence faltered. 'Do, by all means, experiment,' said the stern gentleman, and turned his attention back to the contents of his cupboards. 'It would be best to get the matter over with at once.'

Florian mustered his resolve, and turned to the nearest mirror. It ran from floor to ceiling, an expanse of cold, glittering glass cradled in an ornate bronze frame. He touched it, and felt only unyielding smoothness under his fingers; no promising insubstantiality, no watery vagueness. He tried the next, a smaller silver-framed thing a few doors down; the same result. Three more there were, clad in gold, crystal and wood respectively, and none of these would oblige him either.

The last was bordered in copper, the metal poorly maintained, for it had turned greenish. In this the stern gentleman was checking the result of his selections. He adjusted, minutely, the hang of his indigo brocade coat, a handsome creation which spilled to his ankles in a flow of silver-traced cloth. His waistcoat was the other way about, silvery etched in indigo, his shirt the kind of bright, pristine white that Florian's could only dream of. He wore dark breeches, white stockings, silver shoes and a fall of lace at his throat, and all in all made a fine figure of envy. For a moment Florian forgot the matter of the sixth mirror, so absorbed was he in admiration.

When at last he noticed himself observed, the gentleman moved away from the mirror, with a cordial gesture of invitation. 'Do, please, try not to get fingerprints upon the glass. I have but just had them all buffed.'

Florian scrubbed his fingers upon his trousers as he approached, though without hope of its availing him much, for they were as dirty as his hands. He did not, by now, expect that the mirror would oblige him, any more than the other five had, but he dutifully set his fingers to the glass. 'I don't suppose,' said he nonchalantly, 'that you are informed as to some other means of escaping this place?'

'If I were, I should have long since made use of it,' came the unpromising reply.

Florian digested that in discouraged silence. 'I suppose it is in your power to tell me where I am got to, at least?' he tried.

'You are in the valley of Arganthael,' said the gentleman. 'The house of Laendricourt, therein, and I do not particularly recommend your going much beyond the gardens.'

Arganthael? Laendricourt? The words were so similar, and yet so different. Intriguing. 'Why should I not go past the gardens?' Florian protested. 'Somewhere out there may be the way home!'

'There is not. Believe me, I have explored the possibility, and at considerable risk to my life.' The gentleman, being now pleased, apparently, with his appearance, turned to give Florian the full benefit of his regard, and what he saw did not please him. His brows came down, and the flickering of candlelight reflecting in his cold grey eyes gave him a most uncongenial look. 'Those will not do, here,' he said, indicating Florian's grubby and worn attire with a gesture both languid and dismissing. 'You will stand out a mile, and beside that you will undoubtedly freeze. I had better lend you something.'

Florian's hand went to his bare throat. 'I had the perfect neckcloth for the occasion, for a little while. What a pity that I ever gave it up.'

This earned him a sharp look, but no response.

The gentleman was busy in his cupboards, rooting among an array of waistcoats, and he did not emerge for some time. When at last he turned back to Florian, he was laden down with at least three waistcoats, two coats of similar length and magnificence to his own, a shirt of moon-silver silk tissue, a pair of pale trousers and four neckcloths, all of them lacy in appearance. Florian could not for so much as an instant imagine himself thus arrayed.

He was not immediately given the clothing. 'Who are you?' said the gentleman, pausing to fix him with a look of strange intensity. 'That hair… I do not quite understand it. You have never been here before?'

Florian made him a bow, the most elegant one he could manage. 'I am Florian Talleyrand, of the Chanteraine Emporium in Argantel.' He did not want to admit that he was only a shop boy, and saw no occasion for doing so.

What he had said to discomfort the fine gentleman he did not know, but there came a snapping together of the brows, and he repeated: 'Chanteraine?'

'The Chanteraines are the last word in both convenience and wonder,' said Florian dutifully, wishing yet again that he could, by now, count himself among them.

'Hm.' The gentleman did not comment, but filled Florian's arms with the heap of garments and stepped away. 'You may make your own selections, I suppose?' he said distantly, and then he was gone, though by no visible means, for Florian still could not see a door.

'Wait — who are *you*?' began Florian, but it was too late, and no response came. He fell instead to examining the beautiful things he had been given, with delight and not a little trepidation. What did he know of finery? How was he to determine which waistcoat would look well with which coat, or neckcloth? He puzzled over it for some minutes, feeling somewhat trepid, until he summoned back his usual insouciance and dismissed the matter. If the high-and-mighty gentleman was displeased with his choices, no doubt something would be said.

He made a strange discovery, during the removal of his own clothes. Tucked into one of the deep pockets of his own shabby trousers was a tiny book, which he unearthed from beneath the candle-stub, the tinderbox, the pencil and the couple of handkerchiefs he normally carried about with him. He had taken its weight and shape for his own little pocket-book at first, but upon drawing it out found it to be peacock-blue instead, arrayed in silk, and quite obviously not his pocket-book at all. It was the book Pharamond Chanteraine had tried to bestow upon Oriane, though how it had got into his pocket he could not imagine, for he distinctly remembered leaving it in a store-box at the emporium.

Curious.

But if Oriane was somewhere hereabouts, it was for the best that he had it; he could at last fulfil his master's order of giving it into her own hands.

Shortly after, Florian stood arrayed in shades of green, though none quite matched the vibrancy of his hair. He had a dark green coat with a tall collar and wide sleeves; a waistcoat rather brighter, all stitched about with swirls; the pale silvery shirt and pale trousers; a spill of pewter-coloured lace at his throat; and a pair of boots sturdier than they appeared, in steel-grey. He looked with new regret at his begrimed hands, and settled for hiding them in the pockets of his coat.

The gentleman came back. A swift, surveying look, and he seemed satisfied, for his brow cleared and he made no comment.

'Thank you for the loan of your wonderful clothes,' Florian said.

'I shall expect them back, and unharmed.'

Florian nodded.

The gentleman's attention was fixed again upon Florian's hair. 'Your mother and father,' he said, musingly. 'They have not... do either of them have similarly...?'

He did not complete the sentence. 'Mad-coloured hair?' Florian said cheerfully. 'Oh, no, and neither of my siblings either. I have often been accused of dying it, but that, I assure you, is never the case.'

'No,' came the thoughtful reply. 'I can see that it is not. I am Ghislain,' he added, whether in belated answer to Florian's apparently unheard question or at random, Florian could not determine.

'Ghislain...?' Florian invited.

Ghislain did not immediately reply. Instead he pointed one long finger at some point over Florian's shoulder; upon turning, Florian found, to his surprise, a frosted glass door. Had it always been there, or was it this moment appeared? Florian made for it very willingly, and only when he had set one foot over the threshold and was halfway through transferring the other did he receive a response.

'Ghislain De Courcey,' said the gentleman, and a sensation of shocked recognition arrested Florian's progress on the spot. But too late, for he was over the threshold, and the next thing he heard was the resonating sound of the door slamming closed behind him.

When he turned back, it was to find that the door was gone again.

CHAPTER TWO

De Courcey.

There could be little doubt that Ghislain was some connection of Margot's, though whether Margot herself was aware of his existence or not was impossible to determine. She had certainly never mentioned any missing relatives, as far as Florian could recall; did that mean that this Ghislain had nothing to do with her, despite the coincidence of his surname? Florian longed to return to Argantel and question Margot on the subject at once, and to this end he did his best to find his way back down to the bottom of the house, and the mirror that had brought him through. But the thick, syrupy light that drenched Laendricourt confused his perceptions. His eyes ached and watered, pierced by the brutal glitter of bright golden light off cold, hard glass. Doors blurred, shifted and vanished before he could reach them, or when he did manage to hurl himself over their inviting thresholds he never found that the rooms beyond resembled the chambers he'd glimpsed through their inviting archways.

He went towards a grand bedchamber hung about with dappled drapes and panelled in wood, but ended up in a glass-walled conservatory abundant with trumpet flowers. He thought he saw a stone-walled storeroom, once, through a high archway, and tried to go in, for he had travelled deep and down and hoped this might carry him back into the cellars. But it melted away as he approached, and he stepped out instead into a ballroom so heavily grown over with roses that he could see little of its walls or ceiling. He turned and went back the way he had come, but the corridor beyond was gone and he came out instead into a room full of mirrors.

The room had too many sides, and the quantity of mirrors made it impossible to gauge its proportions. Everywhere he looked he saw an infinity of depthless glass stretching endlessly away; the effect was dizzying. Florian instantly decided it would be best not to linger long in *there,* but when he tried to retrace his steps he found that the door had once again slunk away, and there were no more in evidence anywhere. Everything was mirrors, and he was trapped.

Moreover, none of the mirrors showed *his* reflection; only each other's.

'All right, then,' said Florian to the empty room, and sat down cross-legged in the very centre of the floor. Someone had inset a mosaic impression of a rose just there, and traced its edges in shadow. It gave him an obscure sense of satisfaction to sit on it. 'I have never met a more ill-natured property,' he said with great indignation. 'All a person can reasonably expect of a house is that it should carry one in the proper manner through a sequence of the usual kinds of rooms, but this is beyond you! If you must be so dreadfully inconvenient then I shall simply sit here and read.' So saying, he drew the little blue book out of his pocket and opened it up.

His performance was only partly bravado. It had actually struck him, as he wandered unproductively through the maddening house, that some of the places he found were not unfamiliar to him. Riffling quickly through the book, he soon found the first familiar scene: those red trumpet flowers against hazy glass walls, playing some unheard melody. And there, several pages later on, was the boot-room, its painted complement of boots and shoes different, no doubt, from the ones he had seen, though just as disorganised. There was the ballroom grown over with roses, and the scullery piled high with dishes; the music-room, the greenhouse... they were all in the book.

He began to turn over its pages with a greater interest, wondering whether all of the paintings contained therein reflected actual rooms in this unfamiliar version of Landricourt. He was soon strongly persuaded that they did.

Who had created such a collection? He was no longer convinced that it was Pharamond's work; perhaps his master had bound the paintings up into a book, but how could he have painted them? For that matter, supposing even that he had not painted them — how had he come by the pictures at all?

Moreover, why had anybody gone to such trouble? For these were no slapdash sketches. The tiny paintings had been created with great skill, each chamber of Laendricourt brought to life in mesmerising detail. Florian paused at a rendition of a small library, through which he remembered passing himself at one point earlier in the day. It looked almost as he remembered it, complete to the stacks of books overflowing from the bookshelves and piled upon the floor.

How he should like to go to one of these places, and make a direct comparison! The matter intrigued him greatly, for he began to feel that the book was not a mere curio, done for art's sake. The detail was too intricately rendered, the colours too vivid, the collection too comprehensive. Could any book about such a strange, slippery place as Laendricourt ever be mundane?

What a pity it was that he had foolishly got himself trapped. Energised, he sprang up from the floor and marched upon the nearest of the mirrors, a great, oversized article towering far over his head. It was a narrow, skinny thing, and when it finally consented to display his reflection he found that he looked narrow and skinny, too, and a bit stretched around the neck. A disconcerting image. He examined it for some time, optimistically pressing his hands to its cold, inflexible surface in case he should fall through it, as he had done late under the Gloaming of last night. But it would not oblige him, and neither would any of the other mirrors — each different in size, proportion and arrangement to the next, as though it offended them to be too similar to their neighbours.

'Well,' said he aloud when he had at last given up on that idea, 'I never met a more stubbornly unhelpful set of mirrors either.'

They made no reply.

'I suppose I cannot persuade one of you to turn back into a door?' he tried. 'I cannot quite recall which one it was that I came through, but that need not matter. Any door to anywhere will do.'

They made no reply to that, either.

He took up the book again, hopeful that it might contain some clue he had hitherto missed — and, upon flicking through it, found a painting of the very room he was standing in. He had somehow failed to observe before, and that fact made him suspicious, for he *had*, he thought, gone through the collection with great care. How could he have failed to discover it, if it had been in the book all along?

'I hope,' he said sternly, 'that you were not hiding yourself from me before. That would be very rude, would it not?'

The painting vouchsafed no response either, and Florian began to feel that he was come among a highly standoffish bunch. He turned the book around in his hands, examining the painting of the mirror-room from every angle, for it seemed to him that the image blurred oddly as he looked at it, and could not be relied upon to hold to any consistent configuration. Flickers of colour blossomed, wavered and vanished, and would not hold themselves still for his perusal.

'*There*,' he said suddenly, and pinned something within the painting with the tip of his forefinger. It squirmed beneath his touch, but this time it did not slink away, and he was able to observe that it was a book. A rendering, in fact, of the very same book he was holding… the book slithered and wormed its way through its own pages, did it? 'Now, what are you about, tricksy thing?' he wondered.

He saw it all, in a flash. The book was there, indubitably, but it was there in *reflection*. Inspired, he released the painting of the little book from his grip — only half watching as it spun away — and turned the page over. On the other side was that orangery again, the one that seemed filled with naught but trumpet flowers. That would do. He held the book up, allowing the painting to reflect in the nearest mirror.

It did not quite work as he intended, or hoped. The reflected image spread to fill the mirror edge to edge, and from top to bottom, but the mirror's proportions did not allow of an accurate representation of it; the room came out looking too wide at the corners, and waifish in the middle. He tried again through a succession of mirrors until at last he arrived at a handsome, moderately-sized thing clad in a carved, gilded frame. The painting of the orangery filled the mirror just nicely, and everything there looked restored to its proper proportions.

Steeling himself against another disappointment, he walked forward. As he had hoped, the mirror was no longer a mirror, but a door; he encountered no glass, no barrier of any kind, only empty air; and when he had passed through the frame, he found himself in the orangery itself, his nose filled with the pungent perfume of the flowers.

When he turned back, the mirror-door was gone, and the room of reflections had slunk out of sight.

'Interesting,' he declared to the empty room, and stuck the book back into his pocket. His theory, then, was confirmed, and the fact that the book had been in the possession of Pharamond Chanteraine began to interest him very much. And he had not forgotten that his master had tried to deliver it into Oriane's hands. What had he been about? What secrets was the

Master of the Emporium hiding? Another theory began to take dim shape in Florian's mind, and if his enigmatic master had been standing right before Florian at that moment, he would have had some pointed questions to answer. Or, as was more likely, avoid answering, for it was never his habit to take his shop boy into his confidence.

Florian permitted himself a moment's dissatisfied reflection upon this point, and then dismissed his unworthy feelings. No doubt Chanteraine had his reasons.

He strolled around the hot-house for a little while, experiencing a mild reluctance to leave it again, for it was pleasantly warm in contrast with the biting cold that permeated the rest of the house. But it was no good to linger there long; he would find no way home *that* way, nor discover anything more about the mysteries that increasingly occupied his mind. It required a few moments' diligent searching to discover a way out, but at length he found an abbreviated glass door hidden behind a tangle of trumpet-flowers, and opened it at once. He had to bend almost double to fit through, for it was barely half the size of an ordinary door.

On the other side was the music-room.

'Aha!' said he. 'I remember now.' And he took up the book again, thumbing through its pages until he found the painting of that very room. It soon occurred to him that the painting was not only accurate, but eerily so, for it reflected the room in which he was standing down to its very last detail — even the single red rose, plump and fresh, standing in a porcelain vase atop the gleaming piano; the violet-spun rug upon the floor, one of its corners turned up by a careless step; the pearl hat-pin lying, dust-covered, upon the window-sill.

Florian bent and straightened the rug, ensuring that all of its four corners lay once again flat. When he looked again at the painting, this new configuration of the carpet was accurately reflected therein.

'*Quite* interesting,' he declared. 'I like you after all, book. I think we will rub along charmingly together.'

There was a mirror here, too, though he did not know if it would answer his purpose, for it did not reach the ground; it spanned the wall from corner to corner, hanging elegantly over the mantel above the fire. Nonetheless, still determined to retrace his steps to the original mirror if he could, he chose a page from the book that depicted a cellar-room filled with huge wine-jars and held it up.

The reflection spread to fill the mirror, just as it had in the mirror-room some minutes before. It was become a doorway, there could be no doubt about that. But how could he go through it, when it hung four feet off the floor?

'There are no consistent rules to this place,' he reminded himself. 'Everything turns about as it wills. Perhaps I may turn *myself* about, if I will?'

He tried this. First he took the twisted oak stool from before the piano, and dragged it over to the mantel. Then, finding it insufficiently tall, he stole three fat blue cushions from the seat before the window and piled them on top of the stool. A precarious business, climbing up this makeshift mountain, but he managed it, and stepped from there onto the mantel — which, being broad in width and solidly marble in construction, cheerfully bore his weight. He tried, through a (doubtlessly comical) series of ducking and crouching motions to make himself small enough to pass into the mirror, which failed.

'Hm.' He went back to the book, and turned it, so that the vision of the cellar room tilted in the mirror and fell sideways.

Then, by some method he did not fully understand, Florian tilted himself until *he* fell sideways, and the mirror now being a tall, thin thing instead of a wide, narrow thing, he strolled through it with all the nonchalance of a fellow for whom such sideways-tumblings were the most natural thing in the world. He did not glance backwards, to find the music-room turned all side-about behind him; such a view would only disorient him.

He emerged into the cellar to find the stone-cobbled floor blessedly firm under his feet. There was not much space to walk about in that room, for it was of mean proportions, and was so stacked high with wine-jars that only a few square feet of the floor remained uncovered. They were stacked very neatly, those jars, in a regular pattern that ascended to the ceiling, each stone-made and painted. They were too covered in dust for him to discern any particular pattern rendered upon them; clearly they had not been touched in some time.

A door lay behind him. He peeped through it, and found upon the other side two things: a corridor which looked quite out of place, being brightly-lit and painted all over with a mural of trees. Though they were quite obviously only paint and plaster, the trees rippled in the semblance of a stiff breeze — actually rippled, and swayed, and shivered under the wind! It was no mere illusion, no painter's trickery. The trees seemed to be growing jewels rather than flowers, and each was arrayed in finery of a different hue.

Florian was distracted; but it was not his business to be distracted, not at this time. On the other side of the incongruous corridor — which, he was certain, belonged to some other, quite different, part of the house — he saw another entryway, devoid of a door, and this led into a cellar-room much like the one he was in, only more spacious, and less crowded with wine-jars.

How could he reach it? He was wise to the trickery of Laendricourt by now, and not at all under the impression that he could simply cross the passage and wander into the other room. He would have to try something else.

He backed up as far as he could, and ran three swift steps. A great, flying leap carried him into the corridor, over it, and straight through into the room beyond, without his feet touching the floor at all. Not to any avail, for he did not land in the second cellar-room as he had hoped. He came out somewhere else altogether: a kind of work-room, judging from the three stout, oaken work-benches lined up along the centre. The surface of each was covered in what appeared, to Florian's experienced eye, to be distilling and brewing equipment — the Chanteraine Emporium was well provided with exactly such paraphernalia, with which Pharamond and Sylvaine concocted their elixirs.

Leaning over the middle bench was Ghislain De Courcey, an ancient, frayed robe forming a protective layer over his regular clothing. By his elbow stood a woman unfamiliar to Florian: clad in ivory lace, with a ribbon of indigo at her throat, she had deep-dark eyes and abundant hair. Her arms were folded, and from her posture alone Florian judged that she was in some way displeased with Seigneur De Courcey.

The inelegant manner of Florian's entrance could not help but send up a clatter of noise, and both looked his way.

'Ah,' said Ghislain. 'The young man with the grass got into his hair.'

The lady looked long and narrowly at Florian. 'It has rather, hasn't it?' she agreed. 'A Changeling, do you imagine?'

'No,' said De Courcey briefly, and turned back to his work. 'Born and bred in Argantel, I make no doubt. Only he has strayed into a mirror-pocket at some point in his youth, perhaps, and come out with a little magic got into his blood.'

Florian did not know whether to feel more interested by the topic under discussion, or annoyed that they spoke freely of his probable lineage and history before his very face. 'As far as I know, I was indeed born in Argantel,' he offered, quite as though they had addressed their remarks to him. 'I didn't have much chance to question my parents about it, however.'

De Courcey did not respond. The lady looked Florian over again, and then appeared to dismiss the matter.

Florian's own interest did not so easily subside. He had never before considered that there might be some reason behind the peculiar colour of his hair — as far as he could remember it had always been the colour of grass, and he was not the only person in Argantel with such a characteristic (though the hues did vary). 'What is a mirror-pocket?' he enquired, though doubtful of receiving a response.

The lady ignored it, having drifted over to observe whatever it was that De Courcey was engaged in. But De Courcey, after an interval of silence, did at length speak. 'It has long been known that, should one contrive to trap a quantity of magic in a defined space and surround it with suitably primed mirrors, the effect is to create a never-ending flow. A web, if you like, of magical currents which, endlessly reflected back upon themselves, will tangle and build into a fine little pocket of chaos. Anything finding its way into such a place will not likely emerge unaltered.'

Having just extracted himself from such a pocket, Florian needed no further explanation. He spared a brief thought to wonder what, if anything, had changed about him after that half-hour's adventure. 'But are there such pockets in Argantel?' he said, for he did not remember ever seeing such a place before.

'Your hair,' mused De Courcey, 'is proof that there are. There need not be an array of *glass* mirrors involved, of course, though it is a popular approach if one wishes to build one. Anything that reflects, and that is suitably receptive, will do the job. It has been known to occur at, for example, a confluence of water-ways, should they chance to be ideally arranged.'

'*Ghislain,*' said the lady, in a tone suggesting she had wanted to interrupt for some time. 'Just what is it that you are concocting now? I cannot make it out at all.' She picked up a glass bottle filled with a whitish substance and sniffed it dubiously.

'Do not drink that one, Nynevarre,' said De Courcey. 'You will not at all enjoy its effects.'

Nynevarre hastily set the bottle down.

Florian picked up one that lay upon the bench near his elbow. It had an unusually long neck, and was filled almost to the brim with something viscous and ruby-red. A single bubble formed at the bottom and drifted lazily to the top, whereupon it burst, filling Florian's nose with a sweet scent. He felt sorely tempted to drink.

'Syrup of rosehips,' said De Courcey, glancing Florian's way. 'With one or two things added. Potent. You may sample it, if you like.'

'Is that wise?' said Nynevarre sharply.

'Hush,' was De Courcey's only response, and coolly said.

Nynevarre folded her arms again, and fixed Florian with a glowering gaze he did not know how to interpret. Was she angered with him?

It certainly seemed that taking a sip of syrup-of-rosehips may furnish a range of results, not all of them positive. But Florian was curious, and feeling intrepid after his various successes of the day. And the concoction was appealing, no doubt about it. Its fragrance tugged at him, its colour dazzled his eyes, and he could not help himself. He tipped up the bottle and allowed a very small quantity of it to pour onto his tongue.

Nynevarre quickly took the bottle off him, and set it safely back down upon the bench, watching him closely. This Florian barely noticed, for all his senses were occupied with the business of experiencing the syrup. It tasted like — like honey and wine, like warm chocolate, like summer rain and fresh bread and the berry cakes his mother had used to make, when she was still alive. It tasted, in short, like everything and nothing; nothing in particular, but everything that

Florian had ever loved in his life.

Scents washed over him, the same: the syrup's own, sweet aroma gave way to a jumble of peach-juice and jelly, of mead and milk, of bonfires in autumn and clear ice in winter and the scent of Margot's hair. He felt intoxicated, drunk in a way he had not been in years — and at the same time *not* drunk, far from it. Sharper, in fact, than he ever remembered being before.

'Too potent,' said De Courcey, watching him narrowly. The man shook his head, and sighed, and bent back over his work with a dismissive declaration of: 'Quite useless.'

'I would not say so,' Nynevarre disagreed. 'Not useless at all.'

'He is magic-drunk,' said De Courcey. 'In a moment he will be quite mad, and then he will be himself again, and with what to show for it?'

Florian struggled to focus on the words, for they all fell over each other, and blurred, and in short did everything possible to hinder comprehension. He was sweating, and dizzy; he sat down rather suddenly upon the floor, and held his spinning head in his hands.

He was seeing things. He saw a moonlit copse of ancient trees, a pool of clear water in the centre. He saw an enormous clock with too many faces, hands spinning at impossible speed. He saw a girl who looked like Sylvaine Chanteraine wearing the moth-wing coat, and he saw Pharamond Chanteraine in his work-room, binding up a book. He saw Oriane Travere standing before a mirror, and heard the sounds of clock hands ticking all around her. He saw his employer again, dishevelled and weary, sitting in an attitude of despair upon a bare stone floor. He saw a great many other things, whirling too quickly through his mind for him to grasp their import.

At last the visions ebbed, leaving him shaking and shocked.

'Don't try to get up just yet, my dove,' said Nynevarre, in a far kinder tone than she had addressed to him before. She looked upon him kindly, too, and fussed about him in a manner he found quite agreeable just then. 'You'll be weak for a little while, yet.'

He did feel weak, like his limbs were turned to water. 'W-what was that?' he managed to say.

'That,' said De Courcey in frustration, 'was far too potent. Nynevarre, I do not know what is to become of this mess. Believe me, there is not much I would not do to please you, were it within my power, but what am I to do here? There is no recipe which does not instantly send my poor subjects mad.'

'You are doing fine work,' said Nynevarre soothingly, and winked at Florian.

De Courcey only made a sound of deep disgust.

'Did you see anything of note?' said Nynevarre, to Florian this time.

How could he determine whether anything he had seen was of note? He tried to describe his visions to Nynevarre, but he could not make enough sense of them, and the memories were fading from his mind even as he spoke. He achieved a few disjointed references to arbours and coats and his master, none of which, he could easily perceive, made any sense to Nynevarre. Her face lost its kindly, hopeful expression, and sagged into dismay.

'He *is* rather mad,' she conceded.

De Courcey sighed. 'It will wear off soon.'

Some small part of Florian's mind was still lucid, and crystallised in *that* part was one, clear thought: that this was not quite the first time he had experienced something like this. There had been another time, not long before: when he had found the goldish elixir that Pharamond Chanteraine had sent to Oriane, and stolen a sip.

His lips moved, and after going uselessly through three or four incomprehensible sentences he managed to say: 'Do you happen to know a man called Chanteraine?'

'No,' said De Courcey shortly. 'Save that you have mentioned him before.'

But Nynevarre's eyes widened, and she clutched suddenly at Florian's arm, so hard as to bruise his skin. 'Chanteraine?' she breathed. 'Pharamond?'

'Yes,' said Florian, satisfied.

'*Chanteraine!*' she repeated, and now she seemed angry. 'Tell me where you encountered a man of that name! And tell me, *at once,* where he may be found!'

'Who is he to you, ma'am, if I may ask?'

Her lips tightened. 'My disgraceful truant of a brother.'

Florian nodded, and tucked that information away. Then, watching De Courcey closely, he added: 'And Margot De Courcey? Do you know *that* name?'

Ghislain De Courcey stiffened, turned, and stared at Florian. And now Florian had cause to be a little ashamed of his sensational tactics, for the stern, cool, sometimes grim man betrayed a terrible pain, and an equally terrible hope. 'M-margot?' he said. '*My* Margot? You — you know her?'

'Very well,' said Florian, more gently. 'Please. I

know I am an interloper here, but I am a most unwilling one. As are you, sir, I think? Perhaps, we may be able to help each other.' He added, thinking again of his visions, 'And unless I miss my guess, it may be necessary to help my employer, too.'

Ghislain De Courcey looked at Nynevarre, who still appeared incensed. He looked uncharacteristically uncertain, but *she* growled something incomprehensible, sighed, and said: 'It is high time that *somebody* unravelled this sorry tangle, to be sure.'

De Courcey looked tired. 'Twenty-five years and more have I been stranded here — or is it thirty? I cannot now remember — and I have failed in every attempt. Consider that, young man, and contrive to look less cocksure.'

Florian's optimism was not at all dimmed by this unpromising speech. 'But,' he offered, 'things have changed. You now have me,' upon which words he bowed, and as Nynevarre rolled her eyes and Ghislain De Courcey looked grimmer than ever, he held up a hand to forestall argument. 'We have Oriane, who I am convinced is still somewhere about the place. And we have this.' He took the book from his coat pocket again, and held it up, displaying one of the pages within.

It was the page showing a painting of a workroom, eerily similar to the one in which they were standing.

Now he had their attention. 'Where,' Nynevarre breathed, 'did you get that?'

PART FIVE

MARGOT

CHAPTER ONE

Under the glittering Gloaming, Margot De Courcey walked barefoot from Landricourt into the town of Argantel, singing songs she never remembered hearing before. They were strange, nonsensical songs, but then it was a strange, nonsensical time; not only was the Gloaming early, it was somehow more... well, just *more*.

A day had passed since its first early arrival, and again it had swept over them before its time. Today, only two chimes of the great clock had sounded before the light was swallowed up, and the blue shroud of twilight had covered everything.

Was it supposed to glitter like that? Margot formed the thought in an abstracted way, her mouth still busy forming the words of her melodic oddities as she walked, a basket of flowers and herbs dangling from her arm.

And the mirrors sang, 'Hey-ho, trally-do,
We know the names of the clouds and the snow,
And where it is that the North Wind goes
When the chiming stops and it no longer blows.
And what of the rose that evening brings?
We know the songs that its mirror-heart sings,
We know the stars and the mists and the sky,

We know when magic goes streaming by.

Margot stopped singing, entranced by the vision before her, for she was halfway down the vale and all about her was shadow and shine. It was as though the stars had jaunted down for an evening's entertainment below, and had settled everywhere, anointing each leaf, every flower and blade of grass, with a pale twinkle. The shadows were so deep she could fancy she could fall into them, and never come out again, but the thought did not make her afraid. A current of some kind swept her ever onwards, flowing from Landricourt over the bright grasses and into the town. When she paused and looked back, a thin line showed where she had been: a thin line of darkness, where the stars had gone out.

Thirty-seven years and thirty-seven songs, Margot began again, a different melody leaping to her lips.
Thirty-seven dreams and thirty-seven wrongs,
Thirty-seven faces and thirty-seven lies,
Thirty-seven hours and thirty-seven skies.

She stopped again, for here was someone coming towards her through the mist and the stars, a shadow of a figure she did not recognise, not even when it was almost upon her. But when the woman spoke, she recognised the voice of Sylvaine Chanteraine.

'Who is there?' came the voice.

Margot identified herself, remembering only at the last instant to speak her name, and not to sing it.

'Margot! What are you doing out here?'

'I do not know. I was picking herbs…' Margot ran out of words, for the rest escaped her. What *was* she doing?

'Have you seen Florian?' said Sylvie, in a tone of unusual urgency.

'Not since yesterday.'

Sylvaine gave a sigh. 'I had hoped… you've come from Landricourt? You're certain he is not there?'

'Certain,' said Margot, and hummed a few bars of another song.

Sylvaine stepped closer, and peered intently at Margot. Her hair looked outlandishly bright purple in the weird light of the Gloaming, and her face shone too pale. She looked like some wild, magical creature, and Margot wanted to step back again. 'Are you drunk?' said Sylvaine abruptly.

'Why, no,' said Margot serenely. 'I never touch drink.'

Sylvaine looked her over, rather rudely. 'You *have* come from Landricourt,' she said again, and this time it was not a question.

'I have. Singing all the while.' Having announced which, she proceeded to take up her song again, but was quickly silenced when Sylvaine raised a hand and said sharply: 'Please stop.'

Some small, distant part of Margot remembered that she was not much disposed to wander about singing, as a general rule, and that the evensong of the winemakers was, for her, an exception rather than the rule; this part welcomed Sylvaine's prohibition against further song with relief. But the other compulsion was stronger. Did it come from the Gloaming, too? Was it the stars that brought it, or the flow beneath her feet that carried her across Argantel? She did not know, but it had hold of her; she began to sing again.

Roses are red, and roses are gold,
Roses are stranger than ever was told,
Roses are amber and roses are wine,
They come with the morning and swell on the vine,
But come they in darkness and dress all in white,
Like starlight and moonshine crept in with the night,
Then silver they'll go, and—

Sylvaine had, through much of this verse, been making ever more urgent gestures for Margot to be quiet, and had tried talking over the top of her to no avail. Now she extinguished Margot's song by the simple expedient of clapping a hand over her mouth, which treatment Margot bore in silent astonishment.

'*Will* you be quiet!' hissed Sylvaine.

Margot, her mouth covered, said nothing.

Tentatively, Sylvaine took her hand away. They both waited some time to see whether the verbal flow would resume, Margot quite as interested in the possibility as Sylvaine.

She remained quiet; her songs seemed to be gone.

'Finally,' sighed Sylvaine, and fixed her attention upon the ground beneath her feet. Margot had kept largely to the road on her way through the vale, for it bore the rippling current admirably, and swept her on with it. There was a thrumming beneath Margot's feet which she felt full well considering her lack of shoes. But Sylvaine, shod though she was, appeared to have no difficulty discerning it. 'It is going to be a strange night,' she predicted, and looked hard at Margot. 'It is already, I perceive. Shall I frighten you, if I say that nothing will be as it was, come the morning?'

'Was it so very marvellous, as it was?' said Margot.

'Oh, marvels! We shall have those aplenty.'

Sylvaine said the words disgustedly, and cast an equally unimpressed look at the low juniper bushes that lined the roadsides, each glimmering gently under a mantle of starry motes. 'You had better come with me,' she said. She looked, apparently for the first time, at the basket slung over Margot's arm. 'What are they?'

'I found them on my way,' was the only answer Margot could give. She had scarcely noticed herself picking them, and had carried them off with her without much thinking about the matter. They were jonquil and cherry-bird and wych-elm leaves; blackthorn berries and yellow gentian; pale pasque flowers and lavender and sprigs of linden-branch and who knew what else. Margot had no explanation for them.

'Very well, bring them along.' Sylvaine took up a station to Margot's left and, grasping her elbow in a firm grip, began a march back in the direction of the town of Argantel, propelling Margot along with her. 'There is too much magic abroad tonight,' she said as she walked, heedless of whether or not Margot was hard-pressed to keep up. 'It has got into your head for certain. Perhaps into your blood, too, and if it has not yet then it *will* if I leave you out here.' She sighed and said next, 'There are too many rivers and pools around Landricourt,' as though such a statement followed in any logical fashion whatsoever from what she had said before.

Margot could make no sense of it, but she was not much moved to try. Nothing had made sense since the Gloaming came in, and she found the state more refreshing than frustrating. It no longer mattered to her whether anything made sense or not, and how liberating that was! She wanted to sing again, but mindful of Sylvaine's probable displeasure she managed to suppress the impulse.

Sylvaine was not fooled. 'Please, *don't* sing,' she begged. 'It encourages it, you see. You *ought* to see, given what you are. Why do you think the winemakers sing, when the Gloaming comes in?'

'I do not know,' said Margot truthfully. No one ever questioned the evensong, any more than they questioned the wine-making or, indeed, the Gloaming; it was simply how things were done, in Argantel.

'Not that it has ever worked,' continued Sylvaine, without pausing to elaborate. 'Not with the roses being what they are. But now! Everything will be changed, and who only knows what will come of it.'

'They are red,' offered Margot.

'I daresay they are.'

'And amber, and gold.'

'Yes, yes. Very lovely, and very dangerous, too. There was not that much to object to, the way we were before! It was not precisely *right,* I acknowledge, but it was not wrong either! Meddling fools.' And here Sylvaine fell silent a while, absorbed, apparently, in her own unsatisfactory reflections.

'Rozebaiel is there,' Margot said after a while, moved to offer some new nugget of information into the silence.

'At Landricourt?' said Sylvaine.

'I saw her three times, today. Once in the wine-cellar, once in the ballroom, and once in the tower. She, too, was singing.'

'She does that.' Sylvaine did not sound impressed.

'You know her, then?'

'I know of her. We have not met.' She paused a while, and then added in a grim tone, 'Yet.'

'I don't understand.'

'I don't imagine you do,' said Sylvaine bluntly. 'But you don't need to. There has been a fine mess made, you see, by some of those who went before, and since they have not cleaned up after themselves then it falls instead to some of us who came after.'

'I dislike mess.'

'So do I, but we are to have a great deal more of it tonight.'

Margot looked again at the glittering junipers, and thought privately that if this was Sylvaine's notion of mess then she did not find it so very terrible.

They were bound for the emporium, Margot soon guessed, for Sylvaine led her through the town's west gates — not yet closed against the encroaching night, for the hour was by no means so advanced as it felt — and along the wide Waldewiese. Sylvaine steered Margot unerringly towards the emporium, and at speed. They entered through the back way, straight into the store-room, and Sylvaine slammed and bolted the door against the weird light of the Gloaming, shutting it out completely.

They stood in near darkness for a short while, and then a light flared: Sylvaine had lit a lamp. She turned up its glow until the room was brightly illuminated, then nodded towards the narrow stairwell that led up into the rooms above the shop. 'We're going up.'

Up? Though a regular customer of the emporium — she did not know who was not — Margot had rarely been in the store-room before. She had never at all been invited to explore the rest of the building, and she was not loath to do so now. She made for the stairs — but paused along the way, for her eye had fallen upon the box in which she and Florian had hidden their cache of odd treasures. Had it moved? She could almost have said that it had jumped up, and done its best to catch her eye.

'A moment,' she said, and pointed to the box. 'In there are some things of Rozebaiel's.'

Sylvaine looked sharply at the box. 'How came they to be there? And how came you to know of it?'

'I put them there. And Florian did as well.' Margot thought for a moment. 'It was yesterday,' she elaborated. 'Or perhaps the day before.'

'Aye, time begins to be difficult to follow,' said Sylvaine grimly, and opened the box. She extracted the lovely ribbon without much looking at it, but the moth-wing coat was another matter entirely. When she drew the pile of airy gauze forth, her mouth dropped open and, for some moments, she did not seem able to speak. At length she recovered herself. 'This is not Rozebaiel's,' she said in a voice that slightly shook.

'No,' agreed Margot. 'That one we found in the house of Oriane.'

If Sylvaine heard, she did not reply. She was too busy shaking out the coat, very carefully indeed, and turning it about. 'I am sure,' she was saying softly, 'that it is the same one! Oh, yes — see here,' and she thrust the coat under Margot's nose, pointing to a slight irregularity with the weaving. 'It is the same! How can it be the same?'

'Is it yours, then?' said Margot in confusion.

'In effect,' said Sylvaine. 'It was… my mother's.' So saying, she laid the coat over her own shoulders and slipped her arms into its wispy sleeves. Margot thought privately that it looked made for Sylvaine, for the pretty mauve tint looked custom-matched to her wild hair.

A day or two ago, Margot would have said it was her imagination only that made the embroidery glow like the moon, when Sylvaine put the coat on.

Sylvaine rolled her shoulders and shuddered, suffering under some affliction Margot could not recognise. 'Ah, well,' she said softly. 'After all, then, what choice is there?' On which words she turned resolutely to the staircase and ascended it, calling to Margot, 'I take it back, Margot. Sing as much as you like. Wear the ribbon. We are out of our depth entirely, but what of that? There is no knowing where any of this will go, unless we go along with it. And who knows what might come of it, if we do?'

'Perhaps something bad,' said Margot dreamily, draping the ribbon over her left wrist and tying it there. She noticed, distantly, that the box was almost empty, which did not seem right. Only the little bottle, filled with Pharamond's elixir for Oriane, was left; had there not been some other things in there? Florian's neckcloth, for one. She thought to ask Sylvaine about it, but the other woman was already halfway up the stairs, talking all the while.

Margot put the elixir-bottle into her skirt.

'Yes,' agreed Sylvaine. 'That is the way of everything, is it not? And then, you know, we might also be...' She hesitated. She had gone out of sight, now, and Margot heard only her voice drifting back down the stairs.

'Be what?' prompted Margot, ascending after her.

'Oh, changed!' said Sylvaine. 'But in good ways, not bad. Or in neither, for few things can be given

144

only one label or the other.'

Margot came out at the top of the stairs into a large room which spanned, she judged, the whole width and breadth of the building. Anything she might have said in response to Sylvaine fled from her mind, lost to wonder — and a touch of fear. 'Your father's workroom?' she enquired of Sylvaine.

'The heart of the emporium,' Sylvaine intoned.

The first thing which caught Margot's notice was the windows. There were eight of them, and they were impossible. Not least because each was filled with a single, unbroken sheet of glass, no matter that they were as tall as Margot herself and twice as wide. Such glasswork was beyond the capability of any craftsman, she would have thought. And they showed nothing that they ought. Instead of affording views over the narrow streets of Argantel and their complement of tall, slate-tiled and stone-built houses, they showed variously: a lake of green waters, its surface smothered in lily-pads; an ocean of clouds shot through with lightning; a forest of bejewelled trees clad in russet and gold; a web of rivers and becks, their swift-running waters criss-crossing each other in a veritable maze; a great chamber, ruined, its walls hung with rotting tapestries; a moonlit arbour of ancient, wizened trees; a jumbled village of tall, unusually narrow houses, thatch-roofed and leaning precariously; and a stretch of desert, sands glittering with jewel-dust in every colour.

Three broad work-benches built from stout oak were lined up down the centre of the room, each cluttered with an array of tools. One held brewing and distilling paraphernalia, and was half-covered in bottles, flasks and jars filled with all manner of liquids; one held the tools of a bookbinder's trade, and several partly-constructed tomes; and the third was devoted to some pursuit beyond Margot's comprehension, for she could make no sense of the things that were assembled there. A kind of small, portable loom was one of them, with a length of fabric hanging from it, half-spun. The cloth resembled the ribbon she wore, though it was nowhere near so fine, nor so impossibly beautiful. Three great glass jars stood there also, something misty and insubstantial swirling dreamily inside each one. There was a box full of shards of glass, some coloured, some clear, and all shining softly.

Margot took all of this in with a growing sensation of troubled awe, and said vaguely: 'What in the world is your father up to?'

'Quite,' said Sylvaine, glancing about with the air of one who is so familiar with the contents of a room as to have stopped seeing any individual object long ago. 'That is exactly the question in *my* mind, of late.'

'Of late?' Margot echoed. 'Has he not always been…'

'Strange?' Sylvaine supplied. 'Oh yes, always! And taught me the greater part of his trades. For the past three years and more, I have been the one keeping the Chanteraine Emporium stocked. I mix the elixirs, bind up the pocket-books, bake the sweetmeats and morsels and weave the scarves and the shawls, for father has been too… busy.' She looked at the work-benches, and said with a faint smile, 'This might rather be called *my* work-room, now.' She focused again on Margot, and said in a troubled tone: 'I do not know where he goes, Margot, or what he does. And he has not been seen at all since before yesterday, not by anybody that I have asked. Is it a coincidence, that my father vanishes just as chaos claims us all?'

Margot's head had cleared a little since her walk through the vale. She was able to parse the sense of Sylvaine's words without having to untangle them first, and she could grasp the problem at hand quite lucidly, and without suffering the smallest urge to sing about it. 'I see what you mean,' she answered, slowly. 'But you cannot think that your father has something to do with all of this?'

Sylvaine crossed her arms and stared meaningfully out of the nearest of the windows: the one showing a roiling sea of thunderous clouds. 'Can I not?'

A bolt of lightning shot across that airy sea as Margot watched, and she blinked. 'I see your point.'

'Indeed. So.' Sylvaine began to move about the room with a searching attitude, though what she might be looking for Margot could not guess. She lifted the tapestried drapes and looked behind them; drew up the thick, burgundy woollen rug from the wood-panelled floor and peeped underneath; opened each one of the cupboards that lined the walls and rummaged through the contents. 'I don't know why I am even doing this,' she muttered under her breath. 'It is not as though I haven't searched all these places before, many times over.'

Margot's befogged mind had glided seamlessly over a certain matter before, but now its import hit her all at once. 'You said that Florian is missing?'

'Like Oriane, and like my father. Hasn't been seen by anybody, since the day before last.' Sylvaine did not for an instant pause in her labours as she spoke; rather, her endeavours became almost feverish, and she spun about the work-room like a little hurricane, delving and probing and prying into everything. 'There can be little doubt that they are all vanished by the same means,' she said. 'Well — Oriane and Florian both, I should surmise. My father… I cannot say. Perhaps.'

A knot of worry formed in Margot's stomach, and she bit her lip. Florian was gone, like Oriane, and no one knew where. Oriane had not yet come back. Would Florian, either? Was he in danger? Was Oriane? A sense of helplessness left her frightened and disoriented, and she seized upon Sylvaine's furious activity as a welcome distraction. 'What is it that you're searching for?'

'I don't *know*,' said Sylvaine in frustration. 'My father stopped working in here years ago, so what has he been doing with his time ever since? I strongly suspect that there is somewhere else he goes. I know that he has had some other project in hand, for he has hinted at it before, but he has never consented to tell me anything about it.'

'A secret room?' Margot guessed. 'You think he might have a hidden work-room somewhere hereabouts?'

Sylvaine suddenly stopped, her shoulders sagging. 'It sounds absurd, doesn't it? Where could such a room possibly be hidden? This room we are in fills all the space we have from wall to wall, and the rest above and below is equally well accounted for.'

'Are you certain? Those windows are confusing. We could be several feet from the street and never know it.'

'I've measured,' said Sylvaine ruefully. 'It was one of my first ideas, and I measured very carefully. There is no room anywhere in this house, nowhere that might admit of a hidden space.'

'Right,' said Margot. 'So there isn't a secret room here. What about at home?'

'Father never worked at home, nor would ever bring any of our creations there either. Even so, I have performed the same search, and found nothing.'

Margot went to the window that overlooked the ancient arbour, and stood a moment admiring the trees all silvered with moonlight. 'Are these visions only?' she wondered aloud. 'Or may one step through?' Not that doing so would be wise, were it possible, for they looked down upon the arbour from some vantage point high above; the ground must be some considerable distance below them.

'Visions,' said Sylvaine absently. 'They are only windows, not doors...' Her words trailed off; she bent over one of the work-benches, the one farthest from Margot, intent upon something that lay upon it. 'Now, how odd? I did not know that my father ever painted.'

Margot went to look. A trio of miniature paintings lay atop the smooth wooden planks, each rendered in breath-taking detail. One depicted the emporium itself: the shop floor with its shelves of inviting wares, and the counter behind which Pharamond so often stood. The second showed a room at Landricourt with which Margot was very familiar: the ruined ballroom, holes in its ceiling and roses thick upon its walls.

The third was by far the strangest. It was a large, domed chamber with many sides, windowless, and empty except for an unusually tall clock which stood in the centre. The clock was ornate, built from a reddish wood polished to a mirror-shine and elaborately carved. It had one great, pale face at its top, as was natural, but it also had many more; they were crowded together up and down the body of the clock, all different sizes, and all displaying different times. Margot thought, rather fancifully, that there was a mournful air about the painting, as though the clock were not quite happy about something.

'Oh!' said she. 'I have seen something like these, before,' and she dipped her hand into the left pocket of her skirt. But the book, which she had so carefully deposited in there, was not to be found; nor was it in her right skirt pocket, nor secreted anywhere else about herself that she might have decided to store it. She wondered uneasily how she had lost it. 'I *did* have a book,' she told Sylvaine, 'full of paintings like these, and made, Florian said, by your father. He tried to send it to Oriane.'

Sylvaine looked as though she did not know what to make of Margot's news, or the three paintings either. 'Well,' she said at last, decisively enough, and straightened her spine. 'Since this appears to be the only example of my father's work I have come across in some time, I believe we should consider them important, and take them with us.' She took out her own pocket-book and tucked the paintings in between their pages, handling them very carefully indeed.

Then she paused a moment in thought, and said: 'My father sent Florian into Landricourt, you know.'

'It was mentioned,' said Margot.

'To search for… something. I heard him.'

'Florian did not appear to know what he was meant to look for.'

'I think either my father did not know himself, or

he did not wish to prejudice Florian's mind in any particular direction. What has ever puzzled me since, though, is: why? Why would not my father go himself, if he wanted something from Landricourt? He is ever welcome there. He and Madame Brionnet have been friends for ever, she would not send him away. And he is friendly with all the winemakers. Indeed, for many years he and I were always going there, and poking into every corner of the place just as we liked. Why did he send Florian?'

Margot, much struck, bethought herself of another idea. 'And how came it to be that Florian vanished, so soon afterwards?'

She and Sylvaine looked long at one another, and Margot read the same uneasiness in Sylvaine's face as she felt herself. 'Your father would not…' she began, but was unable to finish.

Sylvaine spoke decisively. 'Deliberately send Florian into danger? Gracious, no! We rely upon that young man for a great many things, and father always said he knew of few so trustworthy, or so dependable. No, if he sent Florian to Landricourt it was because he knew that Florian, of all people, would get the job done. But what was the job?'

'And where has it taken him?' Margot added.

Sylvaine twitched the folds of the moth-wing coat more tightly around herself, and visibly squared herself up to face the inevitable conclusion; one which Margot herself was rapidly reaching. 'It does seem rather like venturing into the eye of the storm,' she said, 'but of course we must go back to the house.'

'I will probably sing again,' Margot warned.

'I imagine we will go singing all the way, and make

fine fools of ourselves. But if there is a reason for everything — and my father has often said so — then there is a reason for your songs, too, and we could do worse than to find out what it is.'

Margot checked that the ribbon was secure around her wrist. Its presence there felt warm and bright and comforting, and she had a sense that she would be unwise to take it off — or to lose it, like she had somehow lost the book. 'To Landricourt,' she said, and tried to speak with confidence.

'To Landricourt,' echoed Sylvaine, and led the way downstairs.

CHAPTER TWO

Outside, the Gloaming reigned still in a state of high glee. The sky was indigo, the clouds were silver, and everywhere was mist and starlight. Margot felt the pulse of magic as soon as her bare feet touched the road: a strong current streaming over the vale, and coming from Landricourt.

There had always been an atmosphere of possibility, of expectation, about the Gloaming: plants stretched out their leaves, lifted their flower-heads to the skies, and grew with frenetic energy; the winds turned cool and warm by turns, snatches of lost melodies swept along with them; it rained, sometimes, out of clear, dark skies, a display presided over by the bright moon and the muted sun all at once. Things were *different,* when the Gloaming came in.

But this was different again. Margot scarcely recognised her own town, for all seemed altered under this intense twilight. It was as though all the magic of Argantel, lost or perhaps asleep, came trickling back when the Gloaming came in — or came sweeping through the vale with a roar, as it had today. The effects — subtle before, and so regular, so ordinary, as to escape particular notice — could not now be ignored.

Margot linked arms with Sylvaine, and they walked, two abreast, back along the Waldewiese and out the western gate. Some way into the vale beyond, Sylvaine paused, and discarded her shoes and stockings. 'That's better,' she muttered, bare skin to the road, and the two women permitted the Gloaming, in all its mischief, to sweep them away.

Ask the wind, sang Margot. *Ask the rain, ask the night,*
Why the mist comes down in the deep twilight,
Why the starlight gleams and the river flows,
Oh! Ask the skies, ask the waking rose.

Ask the wind! sang Sylvaine. *Ask the moon, ask the sun,*
Why the Gloaming comes ere night's begun,
Why the mirrors drift, why the clock-tower cries,
Ask the wind what he knows of the star-drowned skies.

Sylvaine went on, but Margot ceased to hear the words, for something curious was happening which occupied all her attention. There had been but little breeze, when first they had stepped into the street outside of the Chanteraine Emporium. But as they forged onward, growing ever nearer to Landricourt, the wind picked up, and was by now become a powerful force against which Margot and Sylvaine were forced to struggle in order to proceed. And though Sylvaine sang grimly on, unfazed, Margot was distracted, for the wind swept billows of pale, glittering mist before it, and it appeared to her magic-drunk mind that there were faces in it.

There *were* faces in it; she did not imagine it. Or more rightly, there was the same face everywhere she looked: a thin, whitish face, with great, silvery eyes and a mane of starlight for hair. The mouth moved, but if words came forth, Margot heard them not.

This went on for some minutes, and Margot felt that her regard was returned: that if she saw the face, the face also saw *her*. It was fascinated with her, indeed, and with Sylvaine, for those eyes scrutinised them both as it spun about, dervish-like. They were but minutes from Landricourt, and drawn within clear sight of the rambling, beshadowed house, when the dervish calmed, the hurricane of faces resolved into one, solid visage, and suddenly became a man.

'You called me,' he said.

Margot surveyed him in astonishment — or, there was no real surprise; only the feeling that she *ought* to be astonished, and might have been were her blood not fizzing with magic, and the Gloaming all around. As it was, she took in the sight of this abruptly-manifested being with a glad interest. He was tall and waifish, and had an appearance of youth about him. His cheeks were hollow with gauntness, but he possessed an air of energy in spite of this apparent frailty. His hair, mist and starshine, fell in long, long lengths, and it might have touched the floor were it not drifting ceaselessly about, tossed by its own winds. He wore garments spun from the same silver-touched clouds that filled the Gloaming skies, and could easily have melded into them without trace if he so chose.

He returned the dual regard of Margot and

Sylvaine with bright curiosity, and when neither of them spoke he said again: 'You called me. It *was* you, was it not?'

'I believe,' said Sylvaine around a dry throat, her voice a little hoarse, 'that we expressed an interest in asking things of the wind.'

'Why, so we did,' said Margot in wonder. 'And here he is! Shall we be visited by the rain and the night, next, do you think?'

'Or the sun and moon?' said Sylvaine faintly. 'The skies and the rose…'

'I am Mistral,' said the wind.

'That makes sense,' said Sylvaine.

He smiled. 'I do not think the rain or the night will answer, nor the sun or moon, for they are outside the borders of this land of yours, and beyond the reach of your song. But the rose! She, perhaps, we may encounter.'

Margot wondered how it was that the wind had troubled himself to come down upon request, and stand patiently by, awaiting their questions (if they could muster themselves enough to make any of him). But it occurred to her that he was as entranced by them as they were by him, and overflowing with curiosity. He looked about at the darkened, star-drenched meadows, the dusty dirt-road upon which he stood, the clouds overhead and the looming presence of Landricourt behind, and said: 'It is not so very bad, is it? Quite drained, they *did* say, and a misery to visit. But I am pleasantly surprised.'

'It is not usually like this,' Margot felt it necessary to explain. 'These are the Gloaming hours, and much more potently so than is usually the case.'

'I see,' said Mistral, and it seemed to Margot that

he really did see, far more distinctly than she could herself.

'I have a question,' said Sylvaine.

Mistral tilted his head, and fixed all the energy of his attention upon her.

'Why *does* the mist come down in the deep twilight?'

'And for that matter,' added Margot, 'why does the Gloaming come, and swallow up the afternoon?'

'I do not know,' said Mistral with a smile.

Sylvaine was disappointed. 'But the song said to ask you!'

'I did not make the song,' Mistral reminded her gently.

'Neither did we, exactly.'

'Your questions are perhaps too literal,' Mistral suggested. 'Or too exact. Try another.'

'What do you know of Argantel?' Margot said.

Mistral gazed at her. 'I know that it was once another place,' he said softly. 'They called it *Arganthael*, and it was a place of great wonder. Laendricourt stood at its centre, and from within those walls issued forth articles of irreplaceable value to the world.'

'Like the moth-wing coat,' said Margot, with a sudden flash of understanding.

Mistral looked long at the coat Sylvaine wore, as though he had only just taken particular note of it. 'Yes.'

'And?' prompted Sylvaine. 'What became of it?'

'Of Arganthael? It was broken.'

He did not seem disposed to say more. 'Broken?' repeated Margot. 'How?'

'Sundered into two, and none of the mirrors have

157

ever been right again since.'

This could not be made sense of, no matter how Margot tried. 'What have mirrors got to do with anything?'

'We sang about mirrors,' Sylvaine reminded Margot. 'We said that they drift.'

'Oh, they do!' Mistral supplied, with a smile of childlike delight. 'It is quite the puzzle, for they are never where they are supposed to be.'

Sylvaine folded her arms, and looked hard at Mistral. 'Perhaps we could talk to the rose? She might make better sense.'

'Oh, I doubt it.'

'That we could talk to her, or that she might make better sense?'

'The second of those.' Mistral smiled. 'Words are not to be faulted, if their import should fail to be understood.'

Sylvaine visibly gave up. 'I am going to find my father,' she announced, and set off again towards Landricourt.

'Thank you,' Margot said to Mistral, in some little haste. 'I am sorry that we are unable to understand the answers you've been so kind as to give us.'

'You will soon,' said Mistral, with a serene confidence which silenced Margot.

She hesitated, doubting, and then set off after Sylvaine, who strode ahead with her silver-stitched coat flapping behind her.

Margot soon caught up, and they went into Landricourt together. Shadows raced up the great hall's walls as they threw open the doors, letting the starlight in; and it flowed in all in a rush, carpeting the floor with the semblance of thick frost. It covered

Margot's feet, too, though it did not chill her. It felt warm, if anything, and tickled her feet with a faint hum of energy. There was mist everywhere, and someone was singing below.

'Who can that be?' said Margot. By habit, her mind had supplied the name of Adelaide, but it could not be her. She had departed the house at the onset of the Gloaming, with all the rest of the winemakers. Margot had been the last to leave, excepting only Maewen, who never sang.

'Not my father,' said Sylvaine with a twitch of her lips, and it certainly was not he, for the voice was female. But she walked nonetheless in the general direction of the song, intrigued.

'It is coming from the cellars,' said Margot, and thither they went, stealing softly down cold stone stairs into the deeper darkness below. Much was changed along the way. The roses were always abundant under the Gloaming, and it was not much to Margot's surprise to see that they were growing faster and more thickly than ever. They had taken over the doorways and the floors, and seemed intent upon claiming the stairs, too, and venturing deeper than they had ever done before. She was more surprised to see that they had given up their ethereal colour, and blazed forth instead in a host of different hues.

The work of Rozebaiel, Margot realised; but what did it mean?

It was Rozebaiel who sang. She was in the largest of the winemakers' storerooms, humming her lilting, wordless ditties to herself in high enjoyment. The chamber was devoted to the products of last season's labours, wine just a year old, and ready for drinking.

Much of it had already been taken away and sold, but many jars and bottles were left. Rozebaiel had opened them all and was dancing between them; with flicks of her thin fingers and puffs of her own breath, she sent flurries of rose-petals streaming into the top of each bottle and jar, whereupon they promptly dissipated. The wine, as always, was silver-pale, but the petals were crimson and indigo and amber and gold, vibrant with life and magic. The wine looked wan in comparison, and pallid, but flushes of strong colour shot through the liquid with each flicker of Rozebaiel's fingers, until the bottles were filled with wines as blood-red or amber-gold as the flowers she commanded.

'What are you doing to the wine?' blurted Margot, and Rozebaiel's singing abruptly stopped.

'I am mending it,' she said, without looking up, or pausing in her work. 'Don't you see how much better it is? Though it still misses something.' She completed her transformation of the last few jars, and then stood back to survey them, a critical frown creasing her flower-face.

'Much better,' came Mistral's voice, making Margot jump, for she had not realised he had followed them. 'But the final touch lies beyond your power, Rose. Shall I assist you?'

Rozebaiel greeted Mistral's entrance with overpowering eagerness, and all but fell upon him in her joy. 'I knew you would come!' she cried. 'I knew you would not leave me here alone!'

'No, no, I never would,' said Mistral gently, bearing all the ferocity of her love with gentle patience. 'I am late, I fear, for I had to wait an opportunity; the mirrors do not even bend to *my* will, any more. But I am come, little Rose. Shall we finish your work? Then perhaps we may both go home.'

'Home,' repeated Rozebaiel. 'It is so very dull here, my Mistral! Everything sleeps! They are all excessively stupid, and it is tiring labour to wake them up again.'

'But you have done fine work,' said he soothingly. 'I admired it when I came down. How alive everything looks!'

'It is not that I mind, exactly,' Rozebaiel said — perhaps less than truthfully, considering the extent of her indignation before. 'It is wearying for them to keep up the proper raiment, when there is hardly a scrap of magic to be had anywhere. And they are not so *very* dull in that whitish garb, are they? There is even something likeable about it, and perhaps I shall keep a few, when I go home. But so weak and watery! And this wine, the same! Intolerable.'

Mistral dipped the tip of one long, thin finger into the neck of the nearest bottle. A soft wind blew up, making a flurry of Rozebaiel's fallen rose-petals underfoot. When he withdrew his hand, the wine in the bottle had taken up a similar flow and swirled in lazy circles, shot through with the same starry mists that pervaded the rest of Argantel.

'I miss Walkelin's assistance,' admitted Mistral, examining the breath-taking effect he had just created with a dissatisfied air. 'He had always the knack for making a neater weave. But it will suffice, will it not?'

'It is perfect,' breathed Rozebaiel, and she clapped her hands with childish enthusiasm. 'Now do the rest!'

Mistral complied, moving between the bottles one by one. Margot, meanwhile, watched this undertaking in silent awe and total incomprehension, Sylvaine as silent a presence by her side. At length, all the bottles and jars of wine that were in the storeroom were winds-wafted and starry and drenched in colour, and the sight so much dazzled Margot's eyes that they began to water.

'Done!' declared Rozebaiel, with a final, decisive clap of her hands that seemed to proclaim the business quite finished. She turned upon Mistral then, and said, with a mixture of authoritativeness and beseeching charm, 'And now home, Mistral, please!'

Mistral looked uncomfortable. 'Would that I could whisk us both away, little Rose, and without further ado! But the winds have forgotten the way, or perhaps it is closed against us. We must find the mirror through which we came, and go back that way.'

'Oh, the mirror!' said Rozebaiel in disgust. 'Wretched, tricksy objects! It is somewhere here about, I am sure! Sidling from wall to wall, pretending to be *this,* or *that,* and laughing at us all the while.'

'It is somewhere here about, indeed,' echoed Mistral, letting the rest of Rozebaiel's speech pass. His eye alighted upon Margot and Sylvaine, and he developed an expression of faint surprise, as though he had forgotten they were there. 'Do you chance to have seen a mirror somewhere about?' he enquired.

'No,' said Sylvaine.

'It would not, in all probability, look much like a mirror,' he offered. 'At least, not all the time. It might happen to resemble a door, say, or a pool of water, or a window—'

'I saw one turn itself into a vase, once,' offered Rozebaiel. 'A horrid glass vase, all splotched about with the most foolish colours, and sadly ugly besides!

162

And it was no use protesting that it would never dream of being so low an object as a mere a vase, for I *saw* it.'

Mistral smiled apologetically. 'It might also have looked like a vase,' he said to Margot and Sylvaine. He looked upon them with hope. 'You have not happened to see it, have you?'

'Doors we have seen aplenty,' said Margot. 'And a few windows, though whether any of those were mirrors I cannot say. How is it possible to tell?'

'Pools of water and vases?' said Sylvaine. 'No! We have seen none of those. But it might also choose to be a chair, I suppose, or a picture-frame, or a bottle?' Margot heard a degree of irritation underlying her words, and could not blame her, for what kind of answer could be given to so vague a question?

'A bottle!' echoed Rozebaiel, and stared at the many arrayed before her in high suspicion. 'Are you here, Mirror, you abominable thing?'

'Perhaps it were best not to insult it, if you wish for a favourable response,' suggested Mistral in his gentle way.

Rozebaiel merely said: 'It is quite deserved.' She fell into thought, or perhaps daydreaming, Margot could not tell which. Drifting vaguely among the bottles, she trailed her fingers through the roiling crimson liquid of the nearest one and then licked them clean of wine, humming something. Her face changed, and she was silent for a moment before saying, 'Oh, you found my ribbon?' Her bright gaze swept up and down Margot's frame until she spotted the article in question, still tied around Margot's wrist. 'Yes, there it is. I had not even noticed it was gone.' She said this placidly, and made no move to reclaim her property.

'How did you know she had got it?' said Sylvaine, for she, too, had noticed that Rozebaiel's information had apparently not come from her having noticed Margot wearing it.

But Margot knew. The look on her face had reminded her of someone: of Florian, when he had drunk a sip of Pharamond's goldish elixir — the one made from the rosewater and the wine out of Landricourt, and who knew what else besides. Margot had not before been able to account for the odd, distant look on Florian's face afterwards, as though he had briefly wandered very far from her. But now she knew: he had seen something, and so had Rozebaiel. Something, apparently, that had happened; something true.

Pharamond had tried to send Oriane a potion that would show her truths, and he had tried to send her a book of paintings of Landricourt as well. Had he known that she would disappear? Had he been trying to prepare her, warn her, equip her for whatever lay ahead?

He might have. He must have been drinking his own elixirs, too; did they offer visions of future truths, as well as past ones?

'What is the wine?' she said to Rozebaiel. 'Why have we always made it here?'

Rozebaiel did not appear to hear Margot. She had drunk a little more of the stuff, and her eyes had gone vacant again.

But Mistral said, 'It knows.'

'Knows what?' Margot prompted, when he did not elaborate.

'Things that have come to pass, and that are

presently true, and that will come to pass in the future. It is a knowledge it will share, sometimes.'

'It has never done so before.' Margot felt a little disgruntled, for had she not laboured over the rose-wine for season after season, year upon year? Had she not regularly drunk of the fruits of that work, and savoured it, and appreciated it? It had never shared its truths with *her*.

'It would not,' mused Mistral, gazing sightlessly into the depths of one of the jars. 'It is concentrated magic of the purest kind, and you are on the wrong side of the Sundering. Lost all its potency, had it not? A mere flourish of magic at the Gloaming hour can offer little of lasting benefit.'

Margot withdrew Pharamond's little glass bottle from her skirt, and held it up to examine it. It was still nearly full of its goldish potion. 'This is the best your father could manage, I suppose, and not a bad effort either,' she said to Sylvaine, who heard none of this, for she had followed Rozebaiel's example and was sampling the wine. 'Unless it is your work?'

Sylvaine did not answer. She was not really in the room anymore, at that moment.

Margot poured half of the contents of the bottle out onto the floor, and then filled it up from a great jar that stood at her elbow. This one's complement of wind-tossed wine was amber-coloured, and Margot remembered all at once something that Rozebaiel had said a few days before: *You make the amberwyne here?*

'Amberwyne,' she mused, swirling the stuff around in the bottle. The two liquids merged into a pleasing orangey-gold concoction, laced with Mistral's wafts of mist and wind, and Margot gladly took a drink.

It was some time before Margot's wandering mind

returned into the cellar-room.

The visions came at once, and so thickly and quickly that Margot struggled to keep up with the frantic flow of them. She saw some things she had seen before: herself picking up Rozebaiel's discarded ribbon, Adelaide singing, and Florian walking to Landricourt with his odd neckcloth. She saw Maewen Brionnet bending over a vat of half-brewed wine, her aged face creased with sadness, and Pharamond Chanteraine in the work-room Sylvaine had called her own, a paintbrush in his hand, applying the finishing touches to a miniature depiction of a tall clock with too many faces. He, too, looked consumed by sorrow; tears fell from his cheeks and mingled with the paint.

She saw something else, then, that set her heart to hammering in her chest, and filled her with a degree of wonder, hope and rage so powerful she hardly knew how to contain them. Her mind soared farther back, much farther, until she saw a tall, spare man, dark-haired and neatly dressed, whose face she had almost forgotten, for she had not set eyes upon it for nearly thirty years. Her father, who had died. But he had *not* died, she now saw, for there he was in the ballroom of Landricourt, pulling aside a curtain of rose-leaves to reveal a mirror which glowed and glittered in blatant invitation. He touched the cool glass and vanished, and the rose-leaves settled back over a mirror that was no longer there either.

Finally, she saw Pharamond again, but he was younger — her father's age. He had a child in his arms, a little girl, and though her hair was not yet the colour of violets and heather, Margot knew the child to be Sylvaine. He was talking to her, his face worn with care, and she clung to him as though frightened.

Then Margot was back in the cellar-room with Mistral and Rozebaiel and Sylvaine, shaking with shock.

'Pharamond,' she said, when she had caught her breath, 'is not of Argantel, is he? What is on the other side of the Sundering?' She looked rather fiercely at Mistral, who smiled gently.

'Why, Arganthael, and Laendricourt,' he said.

'What are we, some pale, miserable reflection of that place? How mortifying. And Pharamond came from there! I saw him. He wore magic like a cloak. How he has survived in this sad, magicless vale, I cannot imagine. And my father—' Margot's lips trembled upon these words —'My father is gone there, and not dead at all, and what he has contrived to do in a place of pure, condensed magic I do not know either.'

Mistral merely nodded. 'No one ever makes the crossing, but that somebody goes the other way. Some matter of balance, I surmise.'

'So my father went there, and Pharamond was dragged into here, and neither has ever been able to go back the other way.' Margot spoke with a bitterness which shocked her, and she realised there were tears on her cheeks. Her poor mother! They said it was the consumption which took her away, but she had thought herself abandoned, of course, and died of grief and shame.

Sylvaine came near, and Margot instantly said: 'You are not of Argantel either, Sylvaine.'

'Oh, I know,' came the answer, and Sylvaine looked as white and shocked as Margot felt.

'My father is alive,' said Margot.

Sylvaine said, 'My mother is a clock.'

'She… she is what?'

'A clock,' repeated Sylvaine, with every appearance of calm, but her hands trembled, and she breathed too quick.

'The one with too many faces.'

'Yes.'

'How?'

'I don't know! I only saw that she was lost in it — trapped, I think — my poor father! He knew it, and could not get her out.'

'And then you were both stranded here, and my father (and somebody else, I suppose!) lost over there, and what a sorry mess! Your mother must be got out of the clock.'

'And Oriane and Florian and your father got back from Arganthael.'

'And your father too?'

'Perhaps.' Sylvaine bit her lip. 'I did not see him, I do not know if he is there.'

'I saw him,' Margot replied, and described her visions to Sylvaine.

'Both past glimpses. Nothing of the future, or the present.'

'I shall take the bottle.' Margot wiped the glass dry, and tucked it safe away.

She looked up to find Rozebaiel and Mistral observing her with twin expressions of bright curiosity. 'You are going into Arganthael?' said Rozebaiel.

'If we can find the way,' said Margot, crestfallen when she recalled that even these creatures of magic had not been able to spirit themselves home. *And if we can find the way back again afterwards,* she added to herself, for had not her father been stranded in Arganthael for decades? It did not matter. The attempt had to be made.

'The mirror is somewhere hereabout,' said Rozebaiel. 'If it has carried off three poor wretches in three days, then it will carry us, too! You must keep the ribbon,' she said to Margot, quite as though the ribbon and the mirror were closely related in some obvious fashion.

'And the other one has the coat,' Mistral said with approval.

'What of that?' said Sylvaine, glancing down at her splendid garment in confusion.

'It shows the way,' said Mistral. 'You would not wish to end up in quite a different Otherwhere, would you?'

'There are more?'

Mistral smiled. 'Many more. Your father knows a great deal about it, you may find. But the coat knows its way home, and shall carry you safely there.'

'In that case, my own boots may carry me back here again.' Sylvaine admired these articles, though being much scuffed and worn, and their chestnut-leather colour very faded, they did not especially deserve this tribute.

'That *mirror!*' cried Rozebaiel all at once, and indicated, with indignantly pointing finger, a spot on the rough-stone wall which was, as far as Margot could see, quite bare of interest. 'There it was! I saw it, just now! Mistral! It glittered at me, and in a detestably *winking* fashion. And then off it wriggled, and now it is gone again!' Incensed, Rozebaiel stamped her silk-shod foot, and began to mutter a string of invective under her breath. Then she darted for the door, where a few, bold tendrils thick with rose-leaves were creeping around the frame, and took hold of them with both hands. 'The one thing my poor, starved flowers have done well in this miserable place is grow. You have taken it over entirely, my beauties, have you not, and made it all your own? You shall find the mirror for me!' There came a rustling in response, beginning as a whisper and growing to a deep, thrumming *hum* as the roses came awake all across Landricourt. Margot felt the floor shiver beneath her feet. 'Find it and hold it still!' Rozebaiel instructed. 'And I shall come for it!'

Margot jumped as vine-stalks shot across the walls, putting forth leaves and crimson flowers at an astonishing rate. Within a minute or two, all the walls of the shadowy store-room were covered over with them, and the ceiling too. When she walked out into the cellar halls, and looked into room after room, she saw the same thing happening everywhere.

It was not long before Rozebaiel gave a crow of triumph, and cried exultingly, 'They have got it! It is in a big, square room with holes in the ceiling.'

'The ballroom,' said Margot and Sylvaine together. Margot picked up her skirts and ran, Sylvaine just behind her; Rozebaiel and Mistral hurried in their wake.

The ballroom was in chaos. The roses there were in a high passion of some kind, and twisted and writhed about with a furious energy. Margot felt intimidated by them, for each bristled with thorns grown far too long. Not a bit could be seen of walls or ceiling and very little of the floor, for the flowers had taken full possession of this territory. But Rozebaiel marched heedless into the middle of this madness, making her way towards what appeared to be the centre of the storm: a knot of fiercely tangled vines near the top of the wall, where some indignant thing thrashed, and blazed with cold light.

Margot and Sylvaine picked their way more carefully through the litter of thorns, and Mistral merely floated over them.

'Bring it farther down,' ordered Rozebaiel, for the mirror had been lurking very high upon the wall, and was out of reach. With a rustle of leaves it was duly lowered, protesting all the while, and finally fell into a listless sulk at the bottom, its light dimming.

'Excellent,' Rozebaiel purred. 'I could not be more pleased with you, dears.'

The roses preened under this praise, and fluffed up their petals with pride.

'You will let me through,' she told the mirror sternly. 'And *no trickery*!' Without more ado, Rozebaiel laid her hand to the glass and was gone in a flurry of starlight. Only a lingering mist marked where she had stood moments before, and this soon dissipated.

Margot waited, hoping that Oriane might at any moment appear in Rozebaiel's place. But nothing happened. Had Rozebaiel's stern prohibition against *trickery* cowed the mirror so much that it had not ventured upon its usual antic? Or had the pattern broken into chaos, like everything else seemed to be doing?

'I would not delay,' warned Mistral. 'The flowers will not long be able to hold it, without little Rose. Not in this place.'

'If we go through, will someone from the other side end up in Argantel?' said Margot.

Mistral said, 'Perhaps.'

'If they do, the effect will be reversed when we come back, no?' said Sylvaine.

Margot shook her head. 'If that's the case, where is Oriane? Should not the return of Rozebaiel have sent her back to us?'

Sylvaine's eyes widened. 'Oh! What if Oriane has been sent into some different Otherwhere, instead?'

'Make up your minds, and quickly!' snapped Mistral. 'There is not much time.'

Margot and Sylvaine exchanged a look, and Margot saw Sylvaine swallow. She quailed a little herself, somewhere inside, though this feeling she suppressed. 'We must make the attempt anyway,' she said. 'There is no other choice, for what else can we do? Nothing has come of sitting here and waiting.' She strode up to the mirror. Giving herself no time to reflect and doubt and lose her nerve, she set her hand to the glass at once — the hand which wore the ribbon that had been woven in Arganthael.

There was a lurching sensation, and the feeling of plunging face-first into cool water.

And then she was in a cellar again, a darker one than before, and with no roses or jars or anything in it at all.

There was only Pharamond Chanteraine, who sat slumped against the wall near the firmly closed door, looking ragged and exhausted and desperately unhappy. He looked at Margot with blank surprise and said: 'A woman like a rose came through a moment ago.'

'Rozebaiel,' said Margot.

'She turned into a shower of rose-leaves, and was gone.'

'I can well imagine.' Margot looked around at the

172

bleak chamber, and again took in Pharamond's hopeless posture upon the floor. 'How are you, Seigneur?' She noticed, then, that he wore the odd mist-wrought trinket around his neck.

He smiled without joy. 'Defeated, for the present, and I have no glad tidings for you. Hello, my dear.' His gaze shifted away from Margot; Sylvaine had come in behind.

'Father!' said Sylvaine, and went to him at once. 'What are you doing here? Are you all right?'

Pharamond sighed. 'I found the mirror,' he said bleakly. 'At long last! But I came out in here, and cannot leave, and I do not know if I am even got to where I wanted to be.'

'Arganthael?' said Sylvaine, and won for herself a raised-eyebrow look of query and surprise.

'I will ask you how you came to learn that name,' said Pharamond. 'Later.'

A soft wind blew through the room, and mist flew everywhere: Mistral had arrived. 'Ah! Perfect,' said he, smiling broadly, and vanished in another puff of wind.

Pharamond's face brightened with hope and delight upon Mistral's appearance, and fell again when he was gone. 'Elements,' he said disgustedly. 'Not a scrap of sense between them.'

'I suppose he did not realise you were stuck, father,' said Sylvaine. 'And why are you, in fact?'

Perhaps she expected a tale of some magical obstacle or other, some mirror required, or some enchantment necessary; Margot certainly did. But Pharamond only said: 'The door is locked,' and fell to laughing in a hysterical way. 'Thirty years, and I am defeated by a locked door! I have tried every means to open it, and I cannot.'

'Father, you have not been locked in here all day?'

'All day and all night. We are come into some distant store-room in the depths of Laendricourt, I suppose, and no one is ever likely to come into it. There is nothing here.'

'The mirror—' began Sylvaine, but upon turning to look she saw that it was gone again, and sighed. 'I begin to feel as Rozebaiel does, and quite detest those wretched objects.'

'I wish you had neither of you come,' said Pharamond, 'You came in search of me, and Florian and Oriane? I am afraid you have only landed yourselves in insuperable difficulties, as I have.'

'Brace up, father,' said Sylvaine stoutly. 'I am sure we will contrive something—'

The door rattled as she spoke, so unexpectedly that everybody jumped. Then came the unmistakeable clatter of a metal key fitting into a metal lock, and turning, with a groan of protest.

Then the door swung open, and Florian appeared.

'Oh!' he said, and stopped a moment upon the threshold. 'Well, how fortunate. I knew we should find you at last. But what in the world are you all doing in here?'

He turned his sunniest smile upon Margot, who felt that she had never been so glad to see him before, and only refrained from falling upon him in relief due to the presence of so many others. For she could see that someone else was coming in behind Florian, a woman in an ivory dress and with amber-coloured hair.

'We were worried,' she said to Florian, who looked unreasonably gratified by the information.

'Sorry,' he said. 'I had not meant to disappear, you must know.'

'The mirrors!' said Margot disgustedly.

Florian grimaced. 'Bothersome things.'

The unfamiliar woman smiled upon them and said: 'Have we found your friends, then, dove? I am so glad! Only I do not know what possessed them to hide themselves away in here.'

'Nynevarre,' said Pharamond in a half-broken voice.

Her head whipped around, and she studied the prone figure upon the floor in stunned silence. '*Pharamond?*' she finally gasped, then flew instantly from joy to rage. '*Where have you been?*'

Margot, however, was no longer listening, for behind Nynevarre came another person: a tall, spare, silver-haired gentleman in clothes that dazzled her eyes, his demeanour rather forbidding. She did not immediately recognise him either, but in half a moment she saw the traces in his face of another, blessedly familiar and beloved one; a face she had never thought to see again.

'Father,' she said, and the word emerged as a croak.

Ghislain De Courcey looked equally thunderstruck, and it took him some moments longer to recognise in the adult woman before him the little girl he had involuntarily left, so many years ago. But he saw it, and said her name, and then Margot *did* hurl herself upon him, heedless of her audience, and wept all over his coat.

'I do hate to intrude upon all these joyful reunions,' came Florian's voice a little while later. 'But there is some trouble afoot — just a trifle, nothing more!'

'What's the trouble?' said Sylvaine, though without pausing in her unfriendly surveillance of Nynevarre.

'Oh, well,' said Florian apologetically. 'It's only that time is going speedily awry, and the magic is got all out of hand, and half of us are out of our minds over it. And I think, perhaps, that Oriane is in some little danger.'

PART SIX

ORIANE

Something was gravely amiss with the clock.

Oh, it had far too many faces, to be sure; all of them were either too fast, or too slow, and none had the serene, confident air of a clock accurate in its representation of the time. But these were merely the most obvious signs of peculiarity. There were more.

Upon first entering the many-sided room, Oriane had received the impression that the clock was displeased to see her. This she had dismissed as a mere fancy of her own, at least at first; something derived, perhaps, from the clock's immense height, and the way it had of looming over her when she stood directly underneath.

But as the hours dragged by, and nothing happened to release her from the room, she had leisure and occasion to study the clock more closely. She was not required to wind it up again, had she been willing to do so, for it went energetically on, telling all the wrong times, and spinning its minute-and-second hands merrily around its thirty-seven faces. But while the feeling of being unwelcome gradually lessened, the feeling of being observed did not.

When, after some unknowable length of time, the clock began to sing to itself, Oriane was sure.

The clock was aware.

This realisation discomfited her extremely, for a little while. She had had enough of bizarre occurrences. Her tolerance for staircases that wandered off, doors that closed up and re-opened themselves, rooms that were never where they were supposed to be and food that tasted like something else entirely was much depleted; she had no energy to spare for a singing clock that eyed her with a degree of curiosity she could only term impertinent. She longed for the simple comfort and mundane predictability of her own, little cottage, her own plain furniture and warm, sensible clothes, her teapot that meekly poured tea when she lifted it up, and did not presume to disapprove of her, or serve her tea that tasted of cider, or to tire of her and jaunt off somewhere else.

But time moved oddly in the many-sided room. She had the sense, sometimes, that it was dragging itself sluggishly by, every second taking an hour to pass. At others it skipped and burbled and frolicked along, speeding through hours at the rate of seconds. Oriane soon gave up trying to reckon upon how long she had been stranded under the dome of the clock room. She only became increasingly aware of two things: the persistent fear that she would never be released, and an aching loneliness that swiftly grew beyond all reasonable proportion.

Some part of her, then, welcomed the idea that the clock had some awareness of its own, however untoward it may be. Perhaps it could help her to escape. If not, it could at least bear her some company through the period of her imprisonment.

'Hello' she ventured, with a friendly smile. At least, she hoped it was friendly; how did one go about recommending oneself to a clock? 'My name is Oriane, and I'm afraid I am stuck in here. It was not my intention to intrude upon your solitude, I assure you.'

She did not know whether she had really expected to receive a reply, but at any rate she did not. She fancied that the clock's ticking hands sped up a trifle, and spun with a shade more of alertness than they had a moment before; but that was most likely her imagination.

'I do not even know how I came to enter here,' she continued, for it was nice to talk, even without a response. 'I was exploring, and going from room to room with an impunity which has now proved unwise. This terrible house! I knew it derived considerable pleasure from tossing me about, and tumbling me willy-nilly from room to room without displaying the smallest logic or sense. I had not thought, however, that it might carry me somewhere only to trap me, and never let me out again.' She sighed, and sat down against the wall. 'I am trying to bear it bravely but I am growing very tired, and hungry, and thirsty too, and I am afraid I shall starve to death.'

A plate appeared on the floor before Oriane, a delicate specimen decorated with great good taste, and proudly bearing a quantity of fresh bread soaked in butter.

Oriane, astonished, blinked twice. 'I—' she began, and stopped, for more was coming. A glass jug popped into existence, filled to the brim with cloudy yellow lemonade, and there was even provided a cup to drink it from. This little repast was rounded out by an elegant pastry-tart filled with apple preserves, and coated with sugar.

'Thank you,' she said, nonplussed but grateful, and immediately began to eat. She was not much surprised when the bread proved to taste of iced cakes instead, the lemonade of beer, and the apple-tart of (most puzzlingly) salmon. She was too hungry to object, and made a very good meal; the plates and jug were soon empty.

The clock gave a soft chime, and the crockery disappeared.

Oriane pondered this for a while, feeling braver now that she was fed. 'I don't suppose there is any use in wishing for a door?' she ventured. 'Or a window? Any means of exit at all would be splendid.'

There was no mistaking it this time: the clock was clearly engaged in some intense endeavour, and straining hard. It seemed to grow an inch or two, and loomed more grandly than ever. Its faces changed: some grew bigger, and some smaller, and all of the clock-hands spun at dizzying speed.

But no door appeared. All that happened was that a tall, narrow mirror in a silvery frame shimmered briefly into place upon a nearby wall. But it merely sparkled and vanished again a moment later, and the clock sagged back to its former proportions as if exhausted.

'Thank you for trying,' said Oriane politely.

Softly, the clock chimed again.

It had not finished. Something else was in the making, for the clock went first very quiet, and the room filled with a heavy sense of tension and potential; then it became very noisy, chiming and clattering, swaying and clunking, and the hands upon all of its thirty-seven faces spun around backwards, slowly at first, and then at such a speed they became a blur.

Oriane scrambled to her feet and stood with her back against the wall, resolved upon keeping as much distance between herself and the struggling clock as possible. 'Please,' she begged, when the tumult only grew worse, 'do not injure yourself!' And when this entreaty was productive of no alteration in the clock's behaviour whatsoever, she said more loudly: 'What is it that you are trying to *do*?'

The thirty-seven pairs of hands spun and spun and then finally slowed, ticking backwards at a more leisurely pace. When they stopped at last, everything looked rather different.

Oriane herself *felt* different, too. She felt insubstantial, in some odd way, as though she were turned to mist and wind, only held together in any semblance of her old shape by her own will. The room around her bore a different character, for each of its many sides now bore a long mirror. She quickly grasped that these were as corporeal as she seemed to be herself, for they flickered in a ghostly way, seeming more echoes of mirrors that once were, than solid constructs.

The presence of so many mirrors altered the atmosphere in the room, for the light reflected about so oddly that it seemed much amplified, and Oriane's eyes watered until she adjusted to the increased brightness. The light shimmered, too, with a brittle quality that reminded her of the Brightening — though it was not, by any means, the same.

And while the tension in the air had diminished, it had given way to a feeling of heightened energy that was almost intolerable. The floor pulsed with it, the walls shivered, and the air sparked. Oriane's head began to ache.

She counted the mirrors, and found that there were thirty-seven of them... or, no; thirty-six, and one empty space upon the wall.

Then the mirrors washed over with colour, and each blank expanse began to display a scene. Oriane saw such a variety of landscapes as she had never met with before. There was a desert, whose sands glittered as though layered with jewels. There was an ocean of roiling clouds; an exotic forest resplendent with giant flowers; a street full of narrow, tall, thatched houses all jumbled upon on another; a moonlit grove of ancient, wizened trees. There was a vast, scrubby plain baking under a hot sun; a half-ruined palace of white stone, its floors filled with pools of turquoise water; a craggy mountain slope, colonised by white and black goats.

And on it went, through thirty-six variations. Oriane studied each one, fascinated and awed, though when she had completed her perusal of the landscapes she did not feel at all enlightened.

'I do not understand,' she said aloud, and her voice came out thin and weak. The clock was trying to show her something, that much was obvious. But what was it? Nothing yet made any sense.

The last mirror before the empty space — the thirty-sixth — flashed and all but jumped off the wall. Oriane drifted nearer. She soon saw that the ballroom she had briefly glimpsed within, with the murals covering its walls and a great, jewelled chandelier hanging from its ceiling, was familiar to her: it was a vision of Laendricourt itself. As she watched, the mirror's frame twisted and warped, and suddenly it resembled a door's frame instead. A door appeared, too, an expanse of white-painted wood temporarily obscuring the ballroom beyond. The handle turned, and it swung open.

'Oh!' cried Oriane. 'I see! Can I then go through?' And she tried, but of course she could not, for there was no substance to her just at present, nor to the mirror either.

'It used to be a door,' she concluded, and the clock chimed. 'These, then, are all doors,' she said, turning slowly to survey the array of beckoning portals around her. 'All thirty-six of them! Where do they all go?' For only the very last was at all familiar to her; the rest showed landscapes she had never seen and could not have imagined, many so alien they could just as well have led to other worlds.

Perhaps they did.

'But what about this one?' said Oriane, and laid her hand against the bare expanse of wall that separated the first and the last.

In response, there came a great, shattering sound as of a world breaking in two, and the floor shook beneath her feet. Ashen, Oriane clung to the wall, expecting any moment that the ceiling would cave, and bury her in rubble. But it did not. Instead, an insubstantial mirror glimmered into place in that final, empty spot, and it showed another place that she knew: a ruined ballroom, its ceiling gaping half-open, its bramble-covered walls thick with roses.

Landricourt. Argantel. *Her* world.

'Something broke,' she said, and the clock chimed. 'My world split from yours, and fell into ruin.'

She appeared to have guessed aright, for the ghostly mirrors faded away, leaving the walls bare once more. Oriane, restored to substance, paced back towards the clock.

A more intent perusal of its clock-faces revealed something she had not noticed before: a twinned pair, one an obvious copy of the other, and a perfect match for the first save that its glass face was cracked through. It also had, puzzlingly, three clock hands: two which told the time in the usual way, and a third pointing always to three o'clock.

It had, she thought, probably pointed to four, until she herself had come in and interfered.

As she watched, that little third hand quivered, and jumped to point to two.

'Oh, dear,' she said in dismay. 'Everything is got quite into confusion, isn't it?'

The clock chimed, dolefully.

Oriane thought.

'How did all these mirror-doors come into being? Did you make them?'

A soft chime. *Yes.*

'I am sure you did not mean that anything should be broken.'

No.

'And being a clock, and sequestered in here besides, it is hardly to be expected that you should mend it again. I shall be glad to help, for I do like things to be tidy. But how am I to be of any use, when I am trapped in here with you?'

The clock, it seemed, had no answer to make, for there came nothing in answer but silence.

'Did you bring me here? What am I to do?'

Silence.

Perhaps it was thinking. Oriane thought, too, and only came up with more questions. 'Who are you?'

she tried. 'Or, perhaps more rightly, what are you?'

No answer, for a time. And then, just as Oriane was beginning to formulate her next question, she saw a ghost-mirror steal back into place upon the wall before her, and a picture formed within it.

A woman stood there, young and raven-haired. She possessed an air of vigorous energy, and her whole face shone with a confidence and enthusiasm for which Oriane felt a brief stab of envy. She was dressed in fashions Oriane would call outlandish, but which she knew to be common enough in Laendricourt: layered skirts in green and blue, a patterned blouse, and a gauzy, mauve-coloured coat.

The resemblance was not immediately obvious, for the hair was dark, and the face not exactly alike. But it dawned upon Oriane that the woman before her reminded her strongly of Sylvaine Chanteraine.

A second figure materialised in the glass, and Oriane knew it for Pharamond; knew it before the outline of his tall figure was even complete, before the dark colour had seeped into his hair. He was younger by far than Oriane had ever known him, full twenty years younger, if not more. But she knew every line of his familiar face, the curl of his lips as he smiled, the intense quality of his eyes.

'You are the mother of Sylvaine,' she said.

The figures faded from the mirror, and the clock sighed.

With an effort, Oriane set aside all the many implications of this revelation, and kept her mind sternly focused upon the problem she had been offered. To the clock she said, 'Do you know how to mend your world, and mine?'

There was not time for the clock to formulate an

answer, if there was much answer to give, for the sombre quiet in the room as abruptly split apart by a hubbub of voices; there came the sounds of footsteps in quantity, and chatter, and exclaiming in surprise, as several people at once came into the room behind Oriane.

She spun, and there beheld: Florian Talleyrand, sprawled upon the floor as though he had fallen rather than walked into the room, and ended up upon his face; Margot De Courcey, her own friend from Landricourt, looking flushed and surprised and resolved all at once; Ghislain, differently clad from before, and looking both exhilarated and exhausted; and Nynevarre, arm-in-arm with a Pharamond Chanteraine, even as she scolded him.

'Ah!' said Florian, looking up at Oriane from his recumbent posture upon the floor. 'Madame Travere! We had hoped to find you still here.' He glanced with approval at a tiny painting he held in his hand — a painting which, a mere glimpse informed her, depicted the clock-room to perfection — and then held out the picture to Pharamond, who hesitated, but took it.

'I am like to be nowhere else ever again,' said Oriane rather dryly, 'if I am not got out of this room. It has been my prison for the past day at least.'

'Terribly sorry,' said Florian, accepting the hand Margot extended as he picked himself up. 'We would have come sooner, only it took some little time to organise ourselves into a rescue committee.'

'Poor Pharamond had to be rescued first,' said Margot. 'And Sylvaine and I along with him. And *then* we came looking for you. And the clock.'

Oriane had not even observed Sylvaine, for she

had entered the room so closely behind her father and Nynevarre that she had been scarcely visible. She now stood a little to one side, crestfallen and uncomfortable, her attention all fixed upon the clock behind Oriane.

Pharamond had no eyes for anything but the clock, either; not even for Oriane.

Nynevarre was looking around with great curiosity, though her lips were pressed into a disapproving line. 'Aye, my poor dove,' she said, though whether to Pharamond, Sylvaine or someone else was not clear. 'Trapped so long in that clock, and none of us could get anywhere near! The mirrors, you know. Heartless baggages, the lot of them. Flatly refused to get into this spot, and no one but you could have managed it, Pharamond. But where were you? Lost, quite lost! A bad business.'

'Someone else appears to have managed it,' said Pharamond, and *now* he looked at Oriane.

'Yes,' said Nynevarre, and frowned at Oriane as though she were somehow at fault. 'I should dearly like to know how, too.'

'I do not know,' was all the explanation Oriane could offer. 'I did not mean to. I was going, I thought, from one room to another, as I had been all day. But I found myself in here, and then I could not get out again.'

'Some glitch, or oddity,' said Nynevarre, and shook her head. 'The veriest luck! If only it had occurred long ago.'

But the clock did not appear satisfied with this conclusion, for it gave a chime, and shuddered.

'I think she drew me in,' said Oriane.

'She?' said Pharamond, and raised his silvery

brows.

'I know who she is. But I do not know how she came to be trapped in there, or how our — how my world came to be broken off from this one.' The import of everything she had seen and heard came together in her mind all at once, and it occurred to her, halfway through the sentence, that Pharamond was not of her world at all. He came from Laendricourt, and had lived among the people of Argantel for so long only because he'd had no choice.

Oriane looked hard at him. 'Did you make all those mirrors? You and your wife?'

'Thandrian,' he said. 'That is her name. And yes, we made them.'

'You have never mentioned mother's name before,' said Sylvaine, and softly repeated it to herself. *Thandrian.*

'I could not say it without grave pain,' he returned, and the expression he wore as he stared at the clock gave Oriane a sharp pain of her own. 'I tried for more than a year to release her, and to undo what we had wrought. But I failed, and then I was carried away into Argantel — you and I together, Sylvie, when you were but a child. I walked, as I thought, only from my work-room into our parlour, but the door was a mirror, and we never reached the parlour at all.'

'And I was taken into Laendricourt in your place,' said Ghislain, who lingered near Margot. 'Perhaps it was even my doing, for I remember a mirror in the ballroom at Landricourt. It drew me.'

'They do that,' said Florian, with a smile of wry complicity for Oriane.

'They do indeed,' she murmured. To Pharamond she continued: 'What happened? How did you break

Arganthael, and why is Thandrian a clock?'

Pharamond sighed, and looked older than ever. 'It was the work of many years, to create all these mirror-doors,' he began. 'We celebrated each victory, for it was no easy matter. Thirty-six mirrors we built, matched to thirty-six clocks, and they led into thirty-six different worlds. We called them the Otherwheres, and we explored each one as broadly as we dared. It was our intention to throw them open to everyone, when we were certain that they were stable, and safe.

'We grew in confidence, and in power, for so many mirrors assembled all together reflect and amplify all magic. It grows, eventually, to more than the sum of its separate parts, and after we had got so many as thirty-six enchanted glasses together, we... we felt invincible, I suppose. Like there was nothing we could not do, no distance we could not reach past.

'We went further than we ever had before, tried to forge a link with a world much farther off. And we failed. It got away from us, somehow, all the magic we had so carefully nurtured. It twisted upon itself, and the world cracked in two. One half retained all the magic of both, amplified beyond all proportion and condensed into too confined a space; and the other half lost every drop of magic, every whisper, and withered away.

'The mirrors were twisted, too. They would no longer answer when we called, would not obey instructions. They took too much of our magics into themselves, became tricksy and mischievous. And so they still are.'

'Blackguards,' said Ghislain darkly.

Here Pharamond paused, and looked long at the clock. 'My wife — Thandrian — thought to use the clock to mend things. It was our tool all along, the means by which we kept track of our thirty-six worlds, the focus of all the magic we had brought to bear upon the project. It kept the mirrors in check, ensured that we were never too long adrift in the Otherwheres to venture back — it did everything. But it did not have power enough to reverse the ill effects of our mistakes, not when the clock was half broken and the mirrors were slipping away. Thandrian thought to lend it all her own power, and use it to wrest our splintered worlds back into harmony. But the clock simply… absorbed her. She never came out.

'I might have gone in after her, had I not had Sylvie to care for. But there was Sylvie, and I knew Thandrian would never forgive me if I… if I followed her, and never came out either. I tried everything I could, short of that, until I was sundered from her. And I have been waiting for a mirror ever since.'

There followed a tumult, as everybody spoke at once. Some had recriminations to offer (mostly Sylvaine); some had advice to give or suggestions to make (Ghislain, and — loudly — Nynevarre); some offered comfort (specifically, Margot). Only Florian and Oriane were silent, and Florian's demeanour suggested that his mind was as busy as Oriane's.

She drifted nearer. 'You look as though you might have some bright ideas.'

He smiled. 'As do you.'

'Will you tell me yours? And I will share mine.'

'I think we must bring all the mirrors back.'

Oriane nodded. 'Thandrian's plan was probably sound, do you not think? Only she could not do it alone.'

'The mirrors will help, if we can only gather them

up, and then…'

'Then some of us must help Thandrian.'

Florian nodded thoughtfully. 'But how to recall the mirrors, if even their creators cannot?'

'The elements,' said Margot incomprehensibly, who had come up in time to hear most of their conversation. Only she said the word with emphasis, as though it meant more than was apparent.

Florian tilted his head at her in a silent question.

'Rozebaiel,' she explained, which did not much enlighten Oriane but appeared to be of more use to Florian. 'They're… manifestations, aren't they? Pure magic! Rozebaiel and Mistral wrestled a mirror into obedience between them. We all came through it. And somehow, it worked more as it should, without dragging people the other way again. I am sure they could help us.'

'Pure magic,' mused Florian. 'That sounds helpful, indeed.'

The plan soon became a general one, once the hubbub of excitement had died down. Nynevarre was overjoyed to learn of Rozebaiel's return, and promptly said: 'I will find her, the dear. She won't hide from me.'

The aid of only two manifestations was unlikely to be enough, if it had taken the combined efforts of both to subdue a single mirror. But Sylvaine said, 'There are more.'

Margot nodded. 'We sang about them,' she explained, about as comprehensibly as she had spoken of Elements before.

'I see,' said Oriane.

'There is night,' Sylvaine continued. 'And the skies.'

'And the rain, moon and sun,' said Margot. 'That ought to do it, no?'

'Walkelin might be able to reach the sky,' said Ghislain presently.

'But how to reach Walkelin?' said Oriane, whose fruitless efforts to retrace her steps to the Wind's Tower were still fresh in her mind.

'You have his neckcloth,' said Florian, and pointed at the pretty thing around her neck. 'Somehow.'

Oriane had forgotten about it. 'Ah, I do? Very well, then. Perhaps it will lead me thither. And I may find Mistral there, as well.'

Ghislain said: 'Night and moon are often together. With Margot's help, I believe I can reach them.'

That left sun, and rain. 'I will go looking for rain,' said Florian, and added cheerfully, 'It often finds *me*, at any rate, when I am out-of-doors. And if I do not find the rain, it rather stands to reason that I shall instead bump into some sun.'

'I will look for the sun,' said Pharamond.

'No, father,' countered Sylvaine firmly. 'I will go. You are the only person who can reliably deliver us all back into this room, and to mother. You must wait for us somewhere we can easily find you.'

Pharamond's mouth twitched. 'In this house?'

'It's the Brightening, however,' said Oriane. 'It shall not be quite such a chaos. Perhaps the ballroom?'

This proposition was accepted. Only then did it occur to anybody to wonder — Oriane among them — how it would be possible to leave the room in the first place.

'We have this,' said Pharamond, and held up a tiny book. It was filled with paintings, and the one he had chosen depicted the very same ballroom in which he would be waiting. 'I only need a mirror.'

'Can you, Thandrian?' murmured Oriane. 'You would only need to hold it for a bare minute, I think, and perhaps less.'

The clock mustered itself with a whirr of gears and a creaking of aged wood. 'Be ready, Pharamond,' Oriane warned. 'You shall have your mirror in a moment, but it is beyond Thandrian's ability to keep it still for long.'

Pharamond nodded, but barely had Oriane finished speaking when a mirror winked into existence not far away. It wriggled and warped, but it held; with a cry of triumph, Pharamond jumped after it, his book at the ready. Under his direction, the blank glass soon reflected a vision of the ballroom of Laendricourt, drenched in light and high colour.

'Go!' Pharamond cried, and he was obeyed. Sylvaine went through with Florian, first; then Margot with Ghislain; then Nynevarre.

'Quickly,' said Pharamond, for the mirror was writhing about, and threatened to vanish or crack at any moment.

Two rapid steps, and a little leap; Oriane was through. The ballroom was not empty; she emerged into a room full of people, some of whom had doubtless been dancing a few moments before. Music played from somewhere, but the dancers had stopped, to stare instead at the jumbled knot of people who had appeared so abruptly in the middle of the room.

Oriane turned, to watch after Pharamond — and here he came, tumbling out of thin air to land, with admirable grace, upon his feet.

Behind him, an agitated sparkle was all that

announced the presence of the mirror, and it was soon gone.

Oriane thought of poor Thandrian, left once again alone, and wondering, perhaps, if they would ever return for her after all.

We will, she promised silently, hoping that Thandrian would believe it.

And then, to business. 'Right,' she said aloud, ignoring the indignant chatter of the dancers whose revelries they had interrupted. Really, it was far too early in the day to be dancing anyhow! Avoiding Pharamond's eye, she checked that the neckcloth was still secure around her throat, picked up her skirts, and strode for the door.

FLORIAN

It stood to reason that, in order to find the rain, one must first take oneself outside.

Florian tried this.

It was not a simple matter.

'Do you know how I can get outside?' he said to the first person he saw, a large red-haired woman with (inexplicably) ram's horns atop her head. She was seated at the sole table in a large, red-painted room, partaking of the contents of a silver-covered dish which smelled of fish and lemons.

She honoured Florian with an arrogant stare and pointed at the same door through which Florian had just stepped. 'That way,' she said.

'Thank you,' said Florian gravely.

The woman returned to her dinner, and Florian to the door.

He asked the same question of the next person he saw, a small man in a striped blueberry-coloured coat whose hat was almost taller than he was. This red-cheeked little man looked up from tending the oversized flowers that clung to the walls of his greenhouse, and directed a quelling stare at Florian.

'Not through here!' he said in a harsh whisper, as though the flowers might be startled were he to speak too loud.

'Thank you,' Florian sighed, and bowed his way out again.

He went on in this style for some time, wandering from room to room with ever-decreasing hope, until he came to a small room with honeycomb-patterned walls and glass all set into the ceiling. Enthroned within was a stately old woman with bees knitted into her tall, powdered hair, and whose eyes were the exact colour of honey.

She smiled sweetly at Florian.

'Young man, you have the air of the lost,' she said, not unkindly.

Florian might have fallen at her feet with gratitude, for they were the first friendly words that had been addressed to him for the past hour. 'I am trying to get outside,' he explained. 'I want to find the rain.'

She lifted one withered hand, its prominent veins all purple and blue, and pointed. 'That way,' she said with a sickly smile, and there materialised a dainty white door. 'Go that way for the space of sixteen breaths,' she said. 'Or it might be seventeen, I do not altogether recall. Then turn the bluebell way and go on again. You will find the rain.'

Florian was profuse in his thanks. He spent a moment in wondering what the woman did in her odd little room, alone except for the bees; but he dismissed the idea and went quickly through the door, unwilling to lose his passage out now that one had been made for him.

Sixteen breaths. They were among the oddest instructions he had ever received, and he did not know quite how to follow them, for of course he began to breathe differently the moment he was paying attention to it. He tried his best to breathe as he normally would, and counted carefully through sixteen. Along the way, he passed down a garden path of honey-coloured jewels, fringed all about on either side with grasses and ferns. There were tall hedges set a few paces back from the path, so tall that he could see nothing behind them. Each was thick with toffee-brown leaves, and crawling with bees. Their humming filled the air.

At the end of sixteen breaths, he was forced to stop, and stared onward in dismay. There was nothing there, no turning, no alternative path: just the same garden path stretching on and on, and the same tall hedges either side.

Perhaps it *was* seventeen after all, though he did not see how. But he tried it anyway, inhaled and exhaled as he stepped smartly on. And everything changed. The path suddenly veered away to the right, and on the left materialised a glade of drowsy bluebells interspersed with thin little trees.

Florian went that way.

Soon he came to the edge of a wide, still pool. At least, it was mostly still. Its surface was speckled with the appearance of raindrops dripping into the water; but this was puzzlesome, for the sky was still clear and there came not a hint of water falling out of the sky.

'Ah,' said Florian, and stood a moment in thought. He did not see any sign of an Element there, but since it was clearly raining somewhere inside the pool (was it, perhaps, raining from the bottom up, instead of down out of the sky?) he said after a little while: 'Hello, rain. I've come to have a word.'

The droplets stopped.

'Hey!' called Florian. 'Don't make off! I promise I mean no harm! Supposing I *could* harm the rain, which I doubt. And my request is not so very bad, at that!'

'I imagine it is,' came a chill, shivery voice from the air near Florian's left ear. 'But I am bored, so I will hear it anyway.'

The rain was a boy wearing a river for a cloak. He had fog for his hair, and wore a fine, lively deluge for a robe. He regarded Florian out of limpid grey eyes, and waited.

Florian explained.

'Oh, the mirrors,' hissed the rain, and his shoulders drooped. 'They are always getting into my pool, and stirring the waters about.'

'If we are successful,' said Florian hopefully, 'You will not be troubled by them anymore.'

'There is one now,' said the rain, ignoring Florian's words. Looking where the rain so coldly gazed, Florian saw a twinkle under the water, and a spurt of movement like the passage of a big, silver fish.

'You couldn't manage to bring that one along, could you?' Florian ventured. 'We're going to need all of them brought back to Thandrian.'

The rain sighed, took a step, and melted seamlessly into the pool like a bucket of water poured into the sea. When he emerged again a few moments later, he had a mirror in his hands. The mirror was not very happy about this development.

'I know,' sighed the rain. 'But it will be for the best.'

The mirror sighed, too, and went limp, like a length of drowned silk.

Florian led the way back to the ballroom.

NYNEVARRE

Rozebaiel had several favourite little nooks across Laendricourt, but Nynevarre knew which of them she loved the most. It was the same spot in which she had been found, when she had first manifested among them. There was a rose-arbour adjoining the kitchen garden — the roses had been confined there, once, before they had gone mad and claimed all the house instead. Rozebaiel had been discovered there curled under a rose-leaf, a baby no larger than Nynevarre's fist.

Nynevarre knew this, because she was the one who had done the discovering.

'Little rose,' she sang, as she walked that way. 'Your Aunt Nyn has need of you.'

Rozebaiel replied at once, the dear child, as she always did. 'I am here under the leaf.'

She had made herself tiny again, and tucked herself up snugly under a bush. This favoured plant, tended so long by Rozebaiel herself, had been putting out oddly-coloured flowers for some time. It now sported blossoms of every rainbow colour, and more besides, and its thorns were silver.

Nynevarre drew back the leaf, and touched Rozebaiel with one gentle finger. The child looked like a rose herself, diminutive as she was, and wearing her red-petalled skirts. 'Are you well, child?'

'I have had *such* a horrid day!' sighed Rozebaiel as she began to grow. 'What a terrible place is Argantel! I do hope I shall never have to go there again.'

She was back to her proper size by now, and shaking out her skirts, an expression of petulant crossness creasing her little flower-face. Nynevarre wrapped her in a soothing embrace, and murmured calming things. 'Now, my poor dear. I quite understand. But I have a fine adventure for you, and at the end of it there will never again be an Argantel to go into, for it will all be Arganthael once more. Shall you be good, and help your Aunt Nyn?'

'Only tell me!' said Rozebaiel, and Nynevarre did.

By the end of her recital, the rose looked both grim and exultant at once, and made to stride off straight for the ballroom.

'Not just yet, dove,' said Nynevarre. 'The mirrors, remember?'

Moments passed, and the roses rustled. Then Rozebaiel's hands shot out, *one, two*. Glass glittered and sparked, and something gave an indignant shriek.

'I have got two,' said Rozebaiel, and they lay there on the floor before her, smothered in rose-leaves and feebly twitching. 'There shall be more come to us, along the way.'

And off she went, dragging her captives behind her, as ruthless now as she had been forlorn before.

Nynevarre hurried along in her wake.

SYLVAINE

'How does one find the sun?' mused Sylvaine. She had met with a little luck early on, for a chance opening of a random door had immediately offered her the prospect of an exit into the outdoors. It was incongruously placed, for Sylvaine had wandered into somebody's bedchamber, and the door stood directly behind the velvet-canopied bed. But she went through it nonetheless, already growing used to the contortions of Laendricourt, and did not much remark it when the door sidled shut behind her.

There was a wide lawn beyond, recognisably a lawn even if the grass did insist upon being blue. Off Sylvaine went, heavy at heart but full of purpose, and kept her face turned up to the sky.

She could not help grumbling a bit as she walked, for the burdens she carried would not entirely be forgotten. 'And my father *would* neglect to tell me!' she burst out, after a minute's silent trudging. 'Not even my mother's name! And to sit, year after year, and bleat that he could not find a mirror! My poor mama! *I* would have found a way back, if he had only told me. *I* would have stopped at nothing to release her.'

She was lost in such remonstrances as these, spoken to the clear, bright air, when a man materialised beside her and fell into step with her.

It was Mistral.

'I see you are troubled,' he observed.

Sylvaine only grunted.

'Matters are never so bad as they seem?' he said next.

'They are for my mother,' said Sylvaine darkly.

'Are they really?' Mistral sounded intrigued, as though the possibility of anybody's being in genuinely dire circumstances was a new idea for him. 'I wish you would tell me all about it.'

So Sylvaine gave him the whole story, and the plan they had subsequently formed, and was gratified to find that he seemed fully as enthusiastic about offering her aid as she could wish. 'But of course we must free her!' he proclaimed. 'And poor Argantel, too! I never saw so sorry a place in my life.' The winds swirled around him as he spoke, and became a gale; Sylvaine grabbed on to her shawl before it could sail away.

When the winds returned, they bore three mirrors with them, each floating listlessly atop a wisp of cloud.

Mistral patted each in turn, though they squirmed crossly away from his hands. 'Never mind,' he soothed. 'I know it is very shocking of me, but I'm afraid it is necessary.'

'You don't perchance know how to reach the sun?' Sylvaine hazarded.

Mistral did not precisely answer. His face changed, developing signs of tension, and the clouds behind him boiled furiously around their frantically writhing captives. When they calmed, he lifted his head, and howled a word into the air: *'Zoralie!'*

Hurricanes whipped the name away, and Mistral smiled.

A woman appeared. She was gold-coloured, with abundant hair, and eyes that blazed fire. She wore sunlight for her jewels and had bells upon her toes, and sun-silks flared around her as she moved. She was dancing, or had been; she stopped when she saw Mistral, and looked crossly at him. 'What is it now?'

'I need you,' he said.

'Again?' said Zoralie.

'Always.'

Soon they were all three walking back towards the house, Zoralie's quick hands darting out once in a while to grasp something shimmering and incorporeal. The mirrors fought her grip, but with every jerking movement they burst into flame, and subsided at length into a cowed quiescence.

When the group reached Laendricourt, they had seven mirrors trailing disconsolately behind them.

MARGOT

It was Ghislain who found the night, and the moon too.

They had wandered some time without success, for the Brightening bathed the land in such a ruthless glow that no shadow could long survive.

Margot and her father ventured forth from the ballroom, in some confusion as to where they were to go. 'Where does night hide, when the sun shines?' Margot mused.

'He lives in the shadows,' said Ghislain. Margot found it was only she who suffered any confusion, for her father's brisk step and air of purpose proclaimed that he knew exactly where he was going. 'And there are shadows aplenty, in certain parts of this house.'

'Down below?' Margot guessed.

'Exactly. It all goes much deeper down than many realise. There are cellars, and cellars under the cellars, and possibly more cellars under those, too, though I have never ascertained the exact extent of it all. I hope we won't have to.' He led the way through the house with unerring confidence, despite its being, in Margot's perception, a veritable maze of haphazardly-arranged chambers and passageways. Before long they stepped into the first of the cellar-rooms, and shadows promptly crept in among the light. But there was still too much of the latter illuminating the rough stone walls, and Margot was not surprised when her father's brisk step never faltered; on they went, until another staircase led them farther down.

'Why do you need me?' it occurred to Margot to ask, when her father had led them through several increasingly dim passageways, and on to another set of stairs.

'Because,' replied Ghislain, 'The night does not like me.'

'Oh? Why not?'

'I once tried to steal a piece of his cloak, and he has not forgiven me.'

'Steal! Why ever would you?'

'One of my schemes to get home, and he would not share. I am a great favourite with the moon, though,' said Ghislain.

Margot considered it best not to enquire further.

Some little time after that, Ghislain sent Margot ahead, into a large room so dark she could barely see where to put her feet. 'It is safe enough,' her father said in parting. 'There is nothing down here that will hurt you; only do not fear the dark.' And away he went in search of the moon.

Margot found it harder to obey his command than she liked. She had never before thought of herself as a person who feared mere darkness, and had enjoyed many a shadowy ramble across the meadows around her house in search of night-scented herbs. But the quality of the darkness here was different. It was thick and smothering; it drank up all light and swallowed it forever, and some part of Margot's heart refused to believe that she would not be drunk up and swallowed, too.

She ventured forth anyway. Having but just discovered her father still living, she would not begin by giving him the impression that he had a coward for a daughter! But her bravery was sorely tested when, having taken but five or so steps, a voice spoke out of the shadows. It was so deep in tone that its echoes thrummed through the floor, and there was a fathomless quality to it that brought Margot's skin up into goosebumps.

'I am sleeping,' said the voice.

Margot tried for a cheerful note in her reply. 'You seem to me to be awake enough for speech, Seigneur, and for the present that is all I ask.'

There came not a wink of light, but somehow her eyes discerned movement anyway: a stirring of the shadows some way to her left, as of layers of darkness shifting and rearranging themselves.

Night proved to be very tall.

'I d-do apologise for disturbing your rest,' stammered Margot, staring up in growing horror at the imposing figure now looming over her. Everything of him was darkness, from his skin to his long, long hair that writhed and wriggled like shadow itself. He had stars for eyes, and moths nested in his robes. He did not make her any reply, only tilted his head and perused her with faint curiosity.

'I have not seen you before,' he said, and then: 'You are not of this Arganthael, I think.'

'Correct!' said Margot, relieved to arrive at

something like normal conversation with such a being. And she told him the tale of her presence at Laendricourt, as briefly as she could, for what might become of the woman who managed to bore the night?

But he seemed interested, for he asked her a number of questions on some few points of detail; and when she got to the part about the mirrors, and Thandrian, and the sundering of their two worlds, she sensed that she had his attention.

It was not too difficult, after that, to persuade him into joining in their scheme. 'For,' he said, 'the bringing of night to Argantel is so dreary a duty, I have long left it to my deputies among the shadows. And they complain of it to me constantly.'

Margot was a little mortified to hear this indictment of her home, but she would not argue with it. She wondered only what a *true* night might be like, were it brought by darkness itself, and no mere shadow. Perhaps she would soon find out.

There was no sign of Ghislain in the passage, but a girl stood there, about six years old in appearance. She was wan and sickly-looking, though obviously hale enough, for she bounced forward to meet the night with a becoming merriment. Stars drifted in the unearthly glow of her hair, and she wore a pale suit that looked like moonlight on clear water. 'Adventure offers!' she said with charming vagueness, and beamed an irresistible entreaty at the night. 'Father, say we may go!'

To the delight of moon, the night agreed. 'You must bring your toys along,' he ordered.

Moon gaped. 'Toys! But this is an *adventure!*'

'Yes, and for this particular adventure we will need

your toys.'

Moon sighed deeply, exasperated with the bizarre ideas of the night. But she did as she was told, and when, presently, Margot returned upstairs attended by the night and the moon, they had also two mirrors in tow, the moon handling both with the casual skill of a juggler.

ORIANE

Walkelin was pleased to see Oriane.

She was pleased, too, though perhaps more by the fact that she had succeeded in finding him at all. The neckcloth had been of some help, for it appeared to know its way back to its creator and master far better than Oriane. More than once she was prevented from turning the wrong way, by an odd tug upon her neck, or a faint, admonitory tightening around her throat. She was back in Walkelin's presence sooner than she would have imagined possible, though to her disappointment he was alone; there was no sign of Mistral.

'I come to return your neckcloth,' she told him. 'It has been most unhappy to be separated from you, I believe.'

Walkelin accepted it with gratitude, handling it far more gently than either Oriane or Florian had. Oriane wondered guiltily whether it was more fragile even than it looked, and whether she had managed to return it in an inferior state.

Walkelin saw nothing amiss, however, for he smiled upon it, and settled it back around his own neck with something like relief. It suited him better than it had her, though she thought that Florian had worn it with a certain rakish style that could not but appeal.

The weaver was sharp, though, and sensed that Oriane's explanation was insufficient. He watched her with an anticipatory smile, all attention.

'Well,' she said apologetically. 'There is one other thing.'

'Do, please, tell it all to me,' he invited, and she did. She lingered longer than she ought on certain points of the tale — those relating to Pharamond and Thandrian, for example — and felt foolish, hurrying herself hastily on; but Walkelin's regard only grew kinder, and he listened in attentive silence until she had finished.

'Why, I shall be delighted to help you release poor Thandrian,' he said then. 'It is sometimes lonely up here by myself, with only my clouds for company. I shall be glad of an outing.'

Oriane wondered whether he had misheard, or whether she had failed to properly explain her errand. 'We shall be very glad of your aid, of course,' she said politely. 'But I was sent here expressly to entreat your assistance in summoning the sky. The Elements, you see, are the only ones who seem to be able to handle the mirrors anymore—' She broke off, for Walkelin rendered the rest of her speech unnecessary. He closed his blue eye, leaving only the opaque, pearly one open, and winked this second eye at her.

And there was a mirror floating in mid-air, a round sheet of glass that rippled like rain. It got away from him at once, writhing like an eel, but he soon had hold of it again. Little could long withstand the stare of that eye, least of all Oriane.

'You are the sky,' she breathed, mortified. 'Great goodness, I am sorry!'

He opened the blue eye again, and the pressure of his gaze eased. 'I try to keep it quiet,' he explained. 'Or they might not let me Fashion as much as I like. We Elements are not meant to busy ourselves with what they consider the "mundane", you see. What am I to do all day, otherwise? It is all very well to recline upon my clouds, drinking mist-tea and supping upon raindrop-ices, but it does grow wearisome.'

He said all this with a twinkle, and Oriane did not know whether he was telling her the truth, or teasing her. If the latter, she had doubtless deserved it. She was pink at the cheek, but since the sky did not seem to be offended with her, she ventured on.

'You are... do you have any more of those mirrors to hand?'

'They are never to hand,' said Walkelin, looking vaguely about as though one might be seen at any moment. 'But they are often somewhere underfoot. I imagine we will soon discover more, if I put my mind to it.'

'Or your eye,' Oriane murmured.

His smile widened. 'That, as well.'

Oriane found it difficult to meet Pharamond's eye, upon her return to the ballroom. She was glad that Walkelin was disposed to talk. He greeted Pharamond as on old friend — which indeed they were, she soon realised. She heard enough in a short time to learn that Pharamond, too, had been a Fashioner in his

Arganthael days, and to suspect that he was in the secret of Walkelin's real identity already.

He tried twice to speak to her, but she busied herself with keeping her eye on the mirrors, and was not obliged to hear. Several mirrors followed in Walkelin's wake, in a state of great protest; Walkelin had to turn about, and fix them with a quelling glare from his milk-white eye, before they would settle down for a time, and glide along in some semblance of obedience.

'If you are ready?' said Pharamond. 'Everyone else is already gone back, and so we will go in together.'

He had secured a corner of the ballroom for his own use during their absence. The dancers had drifted away, and aside from a few scattered knots of revellers still engaged in conversation, the great room was empty.

Pharamond's mirror was pinned like a butterfly to the wall, writhing in protest. Walkelin silenced it with a look, though it continued to quiver in outrage. A moment's work with the painting was enough to flood its surface with a vision of Thandrian's clock room, and Oriane was encouraged to go first.

In she went.

The room was crowded. She bumped into Florian the moment she emerged from the mirror, and someone else immediately jostled her from behind — Walkelin, perhaps, or Pharamond. She got out of the way as fast as she could, and let her eye run around the room, taking note of everyone who was there. She saw Margot and Ghislain and Sylvaine, and had no difficulty in discerning which of the various Elements there assembled were the sun, the rain, the moon and the night. Rozebaiel was there, and Mistral.

They had formed a tight circle around the clock, and each faced outwards. The walls were covered in mirrors again, though they had not taken up their old positions with any glad spirit; they twitched and shuddered, writhed and muttered, and did their level best to jump off the walls again and slither away. It took the combined efforts of all the Elements to keep them in place.

Walkelin's several — augmented further by the one they had just come through themselves — slunk away to fill the remaining empty spaces upon the walls, and there! The mirror-chamber was itself again, bright with brittle glass.

It did not take long for a feeling of great energy to build in the room, and the mirrors did not like that either. They babbled and twittered, and one of them cracked in half.

'Quickly, now!' Pharamond's voice rose above the noise that the mirrors made. 'This is most unstable, and will not hold for long.'

Oriane was unsure what was meant to happen next, and so was everyone else, for nobody moved or spoke, until at last Walkelin did. He spoke to Oriane alone, in an undertone she was convinced no one else was meant to hear.

'Thandrian will need help,' he said, 'and I think it had better be you. You are the one she summoned, are you not?'

But Sylvaine had already stepped forward, slipping between night and moon in order to reach the clock. She placed both hands against it. 'I do not know what you need of me, Mother, but anything I may do for *you* will be done in an instant.'

The clock chimed.

Sylvaine said, through gritted teeth, 'I *insist.*'

Then she flickered, and was gone.

Pharamond gave a cry of horror, and leapt forward, but too late. No sign remained of his daughter; she was gone into the clock, like her mother before her.

Oriane gathered her resolve. 'I shall go, too,' she said, and before anybody could stop her — *or decline even to try,* her mind insisted on whispering — she did. She needed only to press her fingers to the clock's smooth, polished wood, and the mirror-room vanished. She was somewhere else.

Thandrian had grown older.

The vision of herself she had shown to Oriane was as she had been prior to her imprisonment. She was older than Oriane now, her dark hair liberally sprinkled with white, her face lined with years and cares. She sat alone in the centre of another room much like the mirror-chamber, only this one was so cluttered its shapes or proportions were difficult to guess at. Furniture was stacked up in all the corners, gilded velvet chairs lying crooked under side-tables, or balanced precariously atop chests-of-drawers with half the handles missing. The floor was covered in too many rugs all piled up atop one another, their many colours clashing. Lights glimmered from sconces upon the walls, and lamps hung from the ceiling, but only some of these were functional; many had gone dark.

Thandrian sat atop a towering stack of threadbare carpets as though it were a throne, her back very straight, her chin high. She had all the grace of a queen, though there was a tightness about her mouth and a hard glitter about her eyes. When she looked upon her daughter for the first time in decades, she sat straighter still, and became outright imperious.

'This is the last place of *all* that I should wish to see you!' she cried.

'And it is the last of all places I should wish to see you,' retorted Sylvaine, uncowed. 'Father thinks the same, and how are we to get you out if we all refuse to come in?'

'I am long since resigned to my fate! I only wish to reverse yours, and your father's. Help me in that, and then go away.'

Sylvaine folded her arms. 'What a pretty display of martyrdom! But it will not do.'

Thandrian swelled with rage, and opened her mouth to make some blistering retort. But Oriane judged it best to intervene.

'Pray excuse me,' she said, as mildly but as firmly as she could. 'Had we not better hurry on with mending Argantel, and then decide upon the rest later? The Elements are outside, and they are having no easy time with the mirrors.'

Thandrian deflated again, though reluctantly. She narrowed her eyes at Sylvaine, but let pass whatever she had planned to say. 'The matter ought to be simple,' she said. 'But somehow I cannot get the right thread, or the needle will not properly obey me. I can't think how it is, but I have never managed to stitch up the rift.'

Something about the room had struck Oriane as odd, but it took her until that moment to realise what it was. One half of the room was a near perfect reflection of the other, divided upon a neat line down the middle. The reflection was not exact, for the jumbles of chairs in the corners were not quite the same on each side, and the rugs sported varying patterns and colours across the divide. But that, she realised, was not a bad representation of Argantel and Arganthael themselves.

The rift Thandrian spoke of was a long, straight line cut through all the rugs. It ran under Thandrian's carpet-throne, and it had been messily darned with thick, clumsy stitches.

'What is this place?' said Oriane.

'It is my refuge,' said Thandrian.

Oriane thought she understood. Thandrian had built this room for herself; it was a product of her own mind, in some odd way, and represented her visualisation of the problem. When something was broken, it must be mended, and perhaps she had been handy with a needle, once.

But the solution she had chosen was either misapplied, or she indeed lacked the power to carry it off.

Oriane was still perusing the badly-mended tear in the carpets when Pharamond appeared.

'Oh!' said Thandrian in exasperation. 'That is just what was needed!'

Sylvaine was not more pleased to see her father. 'You should have done this about thirty years ago,' she told him.

Pharamond looked from daughter to wife in silence, unable, apparently, to speak.

Oriane took pity on him.

'Pharamond,' she said. 'You must come and look at this, if you please. It is a clever idea, but I do not think it will answer. Do you?'

Quietly, Pharamond joined Oriane. He needed

only one glance at his wife's intricate labours to agree with Oriane's assessment of it. 'No, indeed. Even supposing the tear could be properly mended—' and he ignored Thandrian's noise of indignant protest — 'there would always be a split here, and the two halves would only ever be joined together, not made whole.' He straightened again, and looked upon Thandrian with wonder tinged with perplexity. 'Is that how you managed the Gloaming, my love? Stitched everything together at the edges, and left the mirrors to it?'

'I *hoped* it would one day suffice,' said Thandrian, no longer angry; all the rage had gone out of her, leaving her drooping with exhaustion. 'If they must reflect, well then, let them reflect some of each land back upon the other! I had hoped it might all balance itself out somehow, even if the rift could not be mended.'

'All this had better come out,' said Oriane, and began to unlace the stitches. Sylvaine helped, and soon the carpets lay once again neatly sundered.

'Perhaps if you did not think of it as carpets,' Oriane suggested to Thandrian. 'Something more easily made whole?'

The carpets dribbled away into the floor, and instead a map appeared, a precise drawing inked upon wood. It was split into two halves by a river that ran down the middle, and it seemed to Oriane that the river — only ink and wood though it was — sparked briefly with the same brittle brilliance as the mirrors. They made a hostile line down the centre of what had once been only Arganthael, reflecting bits of each divided half back upon the other, if imperfectly: light into shadow and vice versa, magic upon the magicless. Far from deriding Thandrian's efforts, she was moved to applaud her. How had she managed to so far regulate this effect as to confine it to a specific hour of the day? She had not been strong enough to make everything right, but that by no means made her weak.

'Water!' said Oriane. 'A thing easily tamed and directed. We might remove it with hardly an effort, I think.'

But though Thandrian had now three supporters to draw upon, as well as the magics mustered by the Elements and their mirrors outside, she could not coax away the water. It ran on, heedless of her wishes, and the two halves remained sundered by it.

The waters filled Oriane's mind, glinting maliciously, and a mirror wriggled in the depths.

'The mirrors,' said Sylvaine. 'They aren't a help. They are in the way. Is there... Mama, is there something wrong with them?'

'They did change,' said Thandrian, frowning. 'After the... accident. They became recalcitrant, hard to manage. They fought me, all the time! It has been terribly hard to keep them in any order, and I *know* they have done things they ought not. Things behind my back, that I never instructed.'

'Dragging people over the divide and swapping them about,' said Oriane. 'Like Pharamond and Ghislain.'

'And lately Oriane and Rozebaiel,' said Sylvaine. 'Florian and Mistral.'

Thandrian growled something. 'I strengthened the bonds, after... after Pharamond. And it worked, for a time. But then I... well, I grew tired.'

'Thirty years,' whispered Sylvaine. 'No wonder you did.'

'Has it been thirty?' Thandrian blinked vaguely at her husband's face, and then her adult daughter's, and her own face fell. 'Yes. I see that it has.'

Oriane remembered winding up the clock, and saw the act in a new light. 'They got away from you again, did they not?' she said. 'The mirrors. They've been tangling everything up more and more, like… like a knotted ball of yarn.'

An appalling thought occurred to her, and apparently, in the same moment, to Sylvaine. Their eyes met, Sylvie's wide with horror. For a moment, Oriane could not speak.

They had been in error. All at once, the hum of energy through Thandrian's refuge ceased to seem promising and began instead to bristle with menace. The mirrors had once been a tool in Thandrian's hands, but no more. They were a menace, warped beyond recognition, no longer the passive and helpful conduit of the Chanteraines' magics.

And what had they done but gather them all together, and merrily turn them loose? So the Elements were watching them: so what? Working all together, building upon each other's powers, they would soon be beyond all hope of control.

The consequences could only be catastrophic.

'We must get out!' cried Sylvaine, and began, frantically, to pace. 'The Elements must stop, let the mirrors go—'

'Let them go?' said Thandrian sharply. 'Why, what have you done with them?'

'Gathered them,' said Pharamond tightly. 'We were to use their power to free you, and mend the rift. All of us at once, and the Elements! A fine plan!' He spoke bitterly, but not even then did his composure waver. 'We have erred, but perhaps it is not too late. We must get out.'

'Get out!' cried Thandrian. 'How!'

No one had any answer to give, and an appalled silence fell.

The hum of energy grew, and turned suffocating. Oriane gasped for breath, panic spinning her mind in useless circles. They'd done the worst possible thing, and could not undo it; and all their friends were at the mercy of the mirrors!

The room shook, the floor trembled, and the sound of tearing fabric rent the air.

'It's too *late!*' cried Oriane, and then a vast, soundless explosion rocked Thandrian's room, and tipped it mercilessly about. Oriane fell, striking the floor painfully, and could only lie there, curled into a shaking ball, as the world frayed, tore, and fell apart around her.

Shrieking, Oriane fell with it.

FLORIAN

Florian soon began to feel that something had gone awry.

He appeared to be the only person suffering any unease, for the Elements were having a fine good time exercising their will upon the mirrors. They took their revenge upon them for every irritation, every inconvenience, every malicious trick the looking-glasses had ever wrought. They drove the glasses before them like cattle, weaving their purloined magics back into a coherent whole, and celebrating their success as the hum of amplified power grew.

But the mirrors seemed far too easily subdued. It looked to Florian as though their show of disobedience was a pretence; compared with their earlier efforts at escape, their struggles now were weak and perfunctory.

The whirl of magics grew until Florian's hair stood on end with the pressure, and his head ached. Glass sparked.

When the singing began, he knew they had gone

badly wrong. The song of the looking-glasses was exultant, and it should not have been. Florian did not perfectly understand what was going on, but that the tables had quietly turned he could have no doubt. The Elements thought they had the mirrors at their mercy, but it was not so; they were at the mercy of the mirrors.

What interested Florian most at that moment was the question of why. What had happened to the mirrors, to twist them so? He did not think for a moment that Thandrian would have designed them thus, or that Pharamond could have wished to create such ill-natured enchantments. Nor had they been described as such, in Pharamond's tale. They had once been a dutiful kind of magic, transporting their creators from Otherwhere to Otherwhere without a trace of mischief. And now they were not.

Was it the effects of Arganthael itself? Laendricourt was much changed by its long duration under disordered magics; perhaps the same was true of the mirrors.

Florian went to the nearest of the thirty-seven glasses, and stared into it.

He did not much expect to see anything of note, but he caught a glimpse of something whirling in the depths of the glass: something he could not make out.

'Here,' said Margot, suddenly beside him. She unstoppered a glass bottle — the same one he himself had once tried to carry to Oriane, it looked like, though the colour of its liquid contents was different — and took a drink. Then she passed it to him, and laid both her hands against the mirror.

'Clever,' said Florian admiringly, and followed suit.

Everything around him fell away, Margot included,

and for a searing instant he was no longer himself; *he was the mirror.* And his whole world pulsed with pain. He felt drunk on it, mad with agony, and could only scream.

A vision filled his mind, colouring his awareness right up to the corners. He felt the great, crashing thunder of magic as Arganthael split in two, was half deafened by the cacophonous noise of it. But even as the valley was sundered into two, the mirrors also broke. Thirty-seven *cracks* splintered his ears one after another: the sounds of glass smashing, like the time Florian had merrily thrown away a boot and then watched, dismayed, as it sailed straight through a window.

The mirrors, warped and broken, drank in magic with in insatiable greed. They were trying to mend, but they could not; they only grew swollen and fat, and sicker than ever.

He snatched his hands away from the glass, unable to bear the pain an instant longer.

Margot was doubled over nearby, one hand braced against Florian's arm. 'They're all broken,' she panted.

'How do you mend broken glass?' said Florian helplessly.

'You don't. It's impossible.'

But Florian was looking at the clock. 'You don't mend them,' he said, 'but what if you could drain all the magic out of them, and make them nothing but glass again?'

Margot caught his meaning immediately. 'Oh, but we are doing exactly the opposite! They are all making each other stronger!'

'Yes, that must be stopped at once—'

Too late, for with a final, unbearable pulse of

magic the mirrors flared so brightly that they burned Florian's eyes, and the world shook around him in a thunder of grinding stone. He fell, hands desperately covering his face as tears poured from beneath his seared lids.

When he was able to open his eyes again, the thirty-seven sides of Thandrian's clock-room were once again vacant. The mirrors had gone.

So, Florian was bemused to note, had moon. And then, all in a tumble, the other Elements vanished, too.

MARGOT

The last thing Margot thought she heard, somewhere beneath the tumult, was the sound of moon's high little voice raised in ear-splitting discontent. It was she who disappeared first, directly after the explosion of power that threatened to split her into pieces.

Then the mirrors had vanished, and that fact struck Margot as odder than all the rest.

But then Margot was vanished, too, all in a flurry. She came out in a serene, moonlit arbour, as composedly seated as though she had been there all afternoon. The scene around her was not unfamiliar: she recognised the twisting curves of the old trees' contorted boughs, silhouetted in the low light; she knew the silvery fruits that hung from their boughs, and felt again the same peace she had known upon looking into the grove before. She had seen it through the window in Pharamond's workshop in Argantel.

And now she was here.

Some things were different from her memory of the place. For one, a small pool of clear, glassy water lay before her, and that had not been there before.

For another, the arbour was no longer a place of quiet serenity, for it was filled with people. All the Elements were present, seated around the pool in a circle. The one they called the skies was stationed to her left; he caught her eye, and winked, displaying no signs of suffering the same disquiet she was feeling herself. On her other side was Rozebaiel, her hands webbed about with stranded silks she was busily knotting together.

There were a few empty spaces around the pool, but these were soon filled. Florian popped up first, looking dishevelled and uneasy. Then came Sylvaine, who glared about herself in high dudgeon, but did not speak. The last place was taken by Oriane.

Margot waited for her father to arrive, or Thandrian and Pharamond, but in vain. They did not appear.

Moon presided.

'This is my *very* favourite place,' she said sternly, and for some reason Margot thought that she was talking to the water. 'You will behave in here, and be good to my friends, or I will make you very sorry!'

She spoke with the authority of a child instructing her dolls in good behaviour, but Margot still could not decide just *who* she was addressing.

Until the pool twitched and glittered, and then bubbled and boiled, and a thrashing commotion sprayed water everywhere, and sent up a billow of steam.

'That is *not* what I said!' bawled moon, and stamped her foot. She waded straight into the pool, until the water flowed up over her knees, and began stomping about in a bristling fury. Glass broke under the water.

'Lunavere,' said night warningly. 'This is no time for your nonsense!'

Moon looked a little chastened. 'Yes, Father,' she said in a small voice, and climbed out of the pool again. She squatted over it, water streaming from her clothes, and touched the surface much more gently. 'Come out,' she crooned. 'I will make you all better!'

A sheet of water rose up out of the water, and hung there shivering as though it were cold.

'Poor, wicked thing,' crooned the moon, and took it. 'It is not really your fault, is it?' In her hands it became a mirror again, though it was not the clear, shining, perfect thing it had seemed to be before. It looked what it was: cracked, tarnished and broken. Moon tenderly stroked it, and then it was not glass anymore, or anything solid at all. It was a puff of mist, or cloud, or something like, which moon swirled around her little fingers and then passed along to the skies.

'Walkelin, you must help me!' she panted, as she plunged her hands back into the water. 'You must all help me!'

And they did, apparently understanding a process which went far beyond Margot's comprehension. Walkelin took the swirl of cloudy something from Lunavere and shaped it in some way, frowning in concentration. When he had finished, he held a frosty cup overflowing with a dreamy blue fog. He paused, frowning at Margot.

'Did you ask these good souls, Lunavere?' he called.

The child was busy wrestling with another of her disobedient toys, but she looked up for long enough to flash an impudent grin at Walkelin.

The fact that this was followed by a guilty look at Margot did nothing to reassure.

'There wasn't time,' she said, a touch defensively. 'But who could possibly mind!' And then she went back to her labours, and not another word could Walkelin draw from her.

The skies looked at Margot. He was obviously troubled by something, but he said: 'She is right, there is not time. I hope you will forgive us.' And he gave her the cup.

Margot understood that she was supposed to drink it. She felt a strong foreboding as to the consequences of doing so, for Walkelin obviously expected that she might have cause to regret it. But the cup shimmered agreeably, a thing of such beauty that she could not help herself; she accepted it. And the dreamy stuff that was pouring from within was so mesmerising, she could not look away. It held all the colours of the skies, and the seas as well, and it smelled of everything Margot loved best.

She drank a sip, cautious. Nothing untoward happened; she was only filled with a delicious warmth which spread right through her, all the way to her toes. It left her feeling both energised and serene, which was a pleasant state, so she drank the rest.

The moment she was finished, Walkelin handed her another.

The same process was taking place around the circle. Night was taking portions of mirror-magic from moon and fashioning them the way Walkelin did, though his concoctions roiled with shadow and gleamed with moonlight. He was giving them to Sylvaine, who received them in her left hand, while accepting cups full of drizzling mist from rain in her right. She drank them down obediently, though her eyes when they met Margot's were rather wide.

Florian was delighting in this peculiar business the way he delighted in everything. Sun was feeding him draught after draught of warm, sparking sunshine, which he guzzled with gusto. He was on the other side of Rozebaiel, who had ignored Margot in his favour; she was stuffing him full of perfumed concoctions which smelled of such heaven that Margot felt a twinge of envy. But a cup of rain's fashioning was put into her hands, and then one each of night's and sun's, and at last one of rose's, too, and she was contented.

Margot began to feel a little dizzy.

'The problem, you see,' said Walkelin softly, supporting her as she swayed, 'is that far too much magic has seeped into this place. Potent magic! We Elements, as they call us, are manifesting faster than ever before, but still it has not helped. And the mirrors, they are drinking it all up as fast as they can.

'Lunavere is a clever child, but there is only so much she can do. She will unwind all the magic, though it costs her dearly to do so, and Thandrian's broken mirrors will be only glass again. But all that magic has to go somewhere, see?'

Margot began to feel that she did see, and her dizziness increased.

'It would have been kinder to you all if we had been able to absorb it ourselves,' said Walkelin, and helped her to lie down in the grass. 'Yes, there, you had better rest a moment. We could not, though, could we? Already we overflow with the stuff; we could not take a jot more.'

'But I could?' said Margot faintly.

'Oh, plenty. Try not to be afraid, for you shall soon feel well again.' He bent over her, his old face creased with concern, and looked deep into her left eye, and then the right. 'Autumn, I suspect,' he said incomprehensibly, and then Margot, gratefully, passed out.

EPILOGUE

Sylvaine had always had wild and unusual hair, but this was something else entirely.

'Is it fire?' she said in a hoarse whisper, her eyes huge with fright. She lifted one hand as though to touch her head, but it hovered a few inches from her hair, and would not be coaxed any nearer.

'N-no,' said Margot, trying to soothe. 'Not precisely. It is more like— like—'

'Thunder,' said Florian. 'If thunder had physical form. With a bit of lightning in it.'

Sylvaine looked down at herself. Her comfortable old boots were gone, as were the rest of her clothes. She wore a gown of roiling clouds instead, motes of lightning blazing in the depths.

'I think you are storms,' said Florian.

Sylvaine said nothing for some time. 'Well,' she said at last, rather heavily, 'That is fitting.' And her lips quirked in her old, wry smile, though they wobbled a bit in the attempt.

Margot had not yet grown accustomed to her new

role either. Not a bit of it. *Autumn,* had said Walkelin, and when Margot had woken up she had soon seen what he meant.

She felt different. She felt, oddly, as though she had no body, though she could see perfectly well that she did. She was too light, her limbs too ethereal; she thought she could float right off the ground if she wanted to, and immediately scared herself half to death by doing so. From her new position twelve inches off the floor, she was in no great state to receive several other realisations equally startling.

Her hair rustled when she turned her head. This was because it was full of leaves, the crisp, russet kind freshly fallen from a waning tree. When she put up a hand to poke gingerly at this unfamiliar mass, she found berries, too. Growing there. In her hair.

Her own garments were fruits and late-blooming flowers wreathed all about in fog, and she smelled fresh earth and herbs and pungent spices wherever she stepped.

Margot swallowed hard.

'Oh, dear…' she sighed, and when Walkelin gave her an encouraging smile she was torn between a desire to cling to this vision of kindliness and wisdom, and a desire to smack him for having landed her in such a predicament at all.

It took her only an instant to surmise what had become of Florian. 'Summer,' she said flatly, and rolled her eyes. 'How appropriate.'

Florian bestowed upon her his sunniest smile. His hair was still green, though it was now shot through with gold, and it occurred to Margot that it probably *was* grass, now. He wore his verdant raiment jauntily, as though it had always been his, and did not even appear to mind the haze of nectar that hung about him. Bees followed him everywhere.

'Was I not made for it?' he said. Spreading wide his arms, he made Margot a bow, and winked at her.

'You could very well have been,' she said thoughtfully, and she was not altogether jesting. 'You take to it well.'

'I am still myself. Only a bit more... magical.'

Oriane's transformation was more puzzling. She had grown grey and pale, which did not seem like her at all. Frost-motes sparkled around her eyes and threaded through her hair, and her gown was a soft flurry of white. She seemed more genuinely cast down by her alteration than the others, for tears shone in her eyes, and she visibly struggled to maintain her composure.

'Winter?' said Margot, frowning. 'That doesn't seem right.'

'Snow, I think,' said Walkelin. 'Her heart may be heavy today, but it is not frozen. *She* could never be so cold.' He went to Oriane and offered her his arm, which she accepted with gratitude. They walked slowly away together.

Moon had exhausted herself. She lay in a spread-eagled heap in the grass, not far from the remains of her pool. There was no water left, only a soggy depression in the ground to mark where it had been. Her eyes were shut, but they flew open again when Margot approached, and she gave her fiendish grin. 'Autumn!' she said in high glee, and clapped her hands. 'It is *always* nice to have new friends.'

Margot felt briefly like kicking the wretched sprite, but restrained herself. Moon had, in all likelihood, saved Arganthael, and there were worse possible consequences to that than Margot's having to wear berries in her hair.

'Is everything well?' she said. 'Is all mended?'

'All better,' Lunavere smiled, and shut her eyes again. 'Go and see for yourself.'

Margot gathered up Florian and Sylvaine, and they went.

'I will never consent to look at another clock in my life!' said Thandrian later, having taken every single timepiece in the whole of Pharamond's emporium and piled them into a heap upon one of his workbenches. She climbed up onto the table and began to stamp them into pieces, smiling fiercely all the while. 'There! Let that be an end to that horrible ticktocking!'

The explosion had greatly weakened the tangled knot of magic that had long held Thandrian bound, and moon's interference had dissolved it altogether. Thandrian had weathered her release from the clockroom well, all things considered. Her hair had gone entirely white, it was true, and she moved with the frailty of one to whom movement had been for too long a rare luxury. But she took such pleasure in it that nobody wanted to stop her, and until she actually injured herself there seemed little hope of her slowing down.

They had all returned to Laendricourt to find everything… changed. The house contained all that had used to be comprised in Laendricourt and Landricourt separately, only now it was merged, and nothing of it was in ruins. The roses retreated, though not altogether, for Rozebaiel would not hear of it. The high walls that used to surround the house and its gardens on the Arganthael side were gone, but beyond their confines lay no dangers; there was only the town of Argantel upon the horizon, just as it ever was.

The Chanteraine Emporium was still in its customary spot, and it had suffered no damage. Later, Margot was to find that her own cottage was just as she had left it, and Florian's too. Not that she was certain they would either of them return permanently to their old homes; where did the seasons live, after all, especially when it was not their turn to preside? But that was for later. For the present, it was enough to know that the sundering was mended, and that there was just as much magic across the house and the valley and the town as there ought to be — and not a drop more. The clock no longer chimed across the valley every afternoon, and the Gloaming no longer came in.

Sylvaine ignored her new status for as long as she could, and revelled instead in her mother's return. They closed the shop for some days, and received only those visitors who had endured the chaos of Arganthael along with them. Margot watched with pleasure as the fractured family slowly mended; as Thandrian regained her health and her strength; as Pharamond remembered how to smile, and Sylvaine delighted in it all.

Only Oriane did not return to Argantel. When she left with Walkelin, she was not seen again at Laendricourt for some time. When she arrived at last upon the eve of winter, she came on the arm of the skies, with starlight in her hair, and she wore her raiment of snow like the regalia of a queen.

It was around this time that Margot stood alone in

her cottage of a home, staring sadly at the things that had used to occupy all of her energy and time. She could no longer gather the herbs or flowers of her trades, for they responded oddly to her presence. They grew, or sometimes they withered. They greeted her with such childlike delight that she could not bring herself to pick so much as a single flourishing leaf. What, then, was she to do? Her old life had quietly folded itself up and gone away, and she had no notion what next to do.

It was in such a state that Florian found her. He knocked cheerily upon her door, and upon her answering it he gave her a smile, and one of his particularly florid bows.

And now his smile really was the sun, thought Margot in bemusement.

'You look bored,' he said.

'I am not bored,' replied Margot indignantly. 'I am only confused.'

Florian nodded thoughtfully, and she could see that he understood all that she had not said. 'Want to go paint the sky?' he said then, and offered her his arm.

'Paint the—! What, will not Walkelin mind?'

'Perhaps he might,' agreed Florian, and his eyes twinkled.

Margot smiled back. 'Why not, indeed?' said the autumn, and accepted the proffered arm.

'Allow me, ma'am,' said the summer, and led her away.

MORE STORIES BY CHARLOTTE E. ENGLISH:

THE WONDER TALES:

Faerie Fruit
Gloaming
Sands and Starlight

THE TALES OF AYLFENHAME:

Miss Landon and Aubranael
Miss Ellerby and the Ferryman
Bessie Bell and the Goblin King
Mr. Drake and My Lady Silver